The Fall
Ch 1

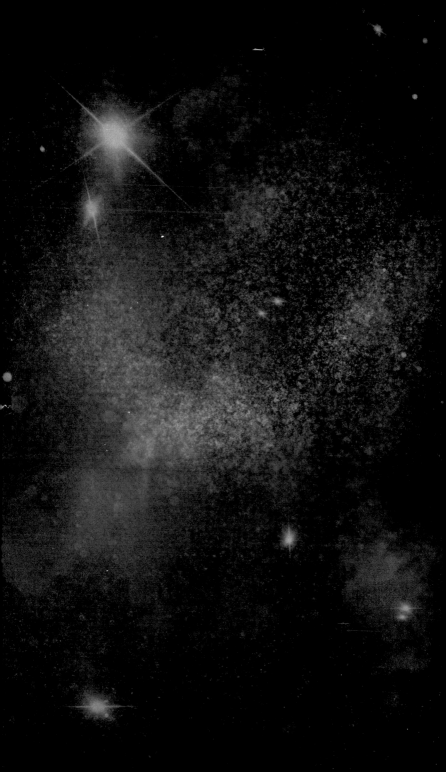

The goddess has your back

Soul Star Sisters

by Jo Stevenson

DEDICATION

To my girls Olivia and Lola
Keep shining brightly

A plea from the goddess

If you're reading these words, you're reading them for a reason.

The universe makes no mistakes.

Ancestors, angels and ascended masters have moved heaven and earth to bring you here, in this moment, to hear this message.

You have been chosen.

Cali wasn't in the library to read; even if she had been, she would never have chosen that book. She was there to hide, and she'd found the perfect spot, tucked behind tall bookshelves at the far end of the mahogany-panelled room. The corner was near the emergency exit and devoid of natural light. If it wasn't for the fact her mum was late, she wouldn't have even been there.

She'd had to think fast and excuse herself from the classroom to escape. As she finally sat at the table, she let out a sigh of relief. She noticed an old embellished book laid open before her. She glanced down at its gilded pages and read:

You have been chosen for a special mission that will save our world as we know it.

We have travelled through time and space to find you.

We are the goddess.

Cali almost laughed out loud. She knew someone who would travel through time and space to find her if she could, and that was Poppy Delongue. Since starting Crestview School just two long weeks earlier, Cali had spent her days taking part in a never-ending game of hide and seek, because Poppy was obsessed with her in a really bad way. It wasn't easy for a caramel-coloured girl with big bushy curls to blend into a quaint independent school in the countryside. She knew she had to learn to keep her mouth shut. Her accent was perfectly normal in London but it now made her sound out of place; like speaking the Queen's English in the middle of a foreign market, where everyone spoke in tongues that she struggled to understand.

Cali's attention was brought back to the book and she continued to read out of curiosity.

The Golden Age was a time when goddesses ruled the entire universe with love, compassion and empathy. People lived in peace and harmony, honouring the cycles of nature, the stars and the moon. Celebrating every single living thing, for all had its special place and unique purpose. But this peace was shattered when a mysterious force took over, creating darkness and division. Chaos and destruction spread like a disease, separating what was once connected, and dividing our world in two.

The world of shadow and the world of the light.

Darkness and disconnection thrive in the shadows. It breeds separation and sorrow, hatred and fear, inequality, bullying and racism. Wars rage in the shadows and they're in danger of destroying humanity and, ultimately, your planet.

We are here to help. We are the goddesses.

The golden hairs on the back of Cali's arms stood to attention. It was almost as if the message was somehow meant for her. If there was one thing Cali despised more than anything it was a bully - she'd attracted enough of them in her life so far. Poppy was the worst kind of bully. She was sly, she was mean, and she tried to make herself feel big by making other people feel small. Ever since that incident where Cali had apparently stuck her nose into Poppy's business, she was now her number one target. Cali hadn't dared to admit it to herself, but something about Poppy made her feel panicky in her chest; she was out of her depth. Maybe she would be better off keeping her nose firmly in this book instead, whatever it was called. She flipped it over to see the front cover. *The Rise of the Global Goddess.* She carried on reading, because right now she needed all the help she could get.

Our magic, just like yours, has always been potent, but also misunderstood. It posed a deep threat to the new order; our sisters were tortured and many went into hiding. Now, the goddesses, holders of ancient wisdom, have been silenced and banished from the earth. The people there live in fear, feeling separate and alone. They can no longer hear our guidance. They have turned against each other and lost all faith and hope. Wars are being fought, driven by greed and the need for power. Our beautiful Mother Earth is being ravaged; she is suffering. The ecosystems and the animals are dying.

Without your help, the world and every living thing in it will be destroyed.

*

For centuries, our stories have been hidden and our power denied.

But it is now time for our voices to be heard. It is time for our sisters to rise.

We can only do this with your help.

You are invited to join forces with the goddesses. You will be guided to unlock your power in the ways of the light warrior and play a unique part in our destiny.

For you are the keepers of the keys, the alchemists, the bridge walkers. You were born to help build the rainbow bridge that will restore balance to your planet and reconnect heaven and earth. To do this, you must travel through seven different coloured realms that will each bring its own quests and challenges. Each lesson you master will awaken your own magic and activate light within you. As you ascend, you will raise the energy and vibration of the planet. When all seven steps have been illuminated, the glorious rainbow bridge will be formed. All of humanity will awaken to the beauty of this light and we will once again live in love, peace and unity.

As above, so below.

Our future is in your hands, for legend has told that the world will be saved by girls like you.

Are you ready to enter our world?

Something strange happened as Cali read the words. A stirring in her belly triggered a whole scene inside her mind of some magnificent world where the light was beautiful and bright.

A high-pitched snigger sliced through the heavy silence of the library, causing the magical movie in Cali's mind to end abruptly. However far away she had travelled her brain instantly recognised the voice and alerted her to the danger, jolting her back to the black typed words on the stark white page. She held her breath in the hope that it might somehow make her invisible.

She instinctively scrambled to pick up her things and stuff them into her bag. She stamped her feet on the floor, furious that the barricade of books had betrayed her, worried her safe space was now under serious threat.

The volume of laughter increased and Cali sensed that the energy in the library had altered and was reflected within her as a sticky, suffocating sensation, circling inside the pit of her stomach.

It reminded her of the slime her little sister liked to play with, and she wondered if this was how uncomfortable it would feel to swallow it. Her mind whirled, questioning whether to stay or leave, and worrying about what would happen if she did either. The intense sensations within her made it difficult to decide and she remained frozen to the spot.

'I know I saw her sneak around here.'

There was no mistaking Poppy's annoying nasal voice, which sounded almost comical - like she was imitating herself. But no, she really was that snobby, that fake.

'She has a lot to learn about how things work around here,' came the response. It was no surprise at all that Martha Thompson was by Poppy's side. They stuck together like macaroni and cheese, literally. Dull, bland pasta, together with its stringy, cheesy topping that may look appealing, but which gives you indigestion after eating it (unless it was made by Cali's grandma, of course, then it was delicious). The two girls strode around the school like they owned it, swishing their matching blonde hair. Poppy's was long with natural sun-streaked highlights; Martha's was shoulder-length with waves. Their perfectly-white straight teeth sparkled brightly against their perpetually-tanned, glowing skin. Their immaculately-applied mascara didn't seem to clump like Cali's did whenever she tried to apply it. Not that she would dare wear it for school - her dad would ground her for eternity.

Cali had watched them from the sidelines. She wasn't fooled by their shiny 'popular girl' act that everybody else seemed to fall for.

Cali inhaled deeply and her mind cleared enough to tell her she had to move. Poppy's voice was getting closer. Without thinking, Cali scooped up the old library book with her coat and bag. She headed straight for the emergency exit. If she was quick, she could slip out of there and avoid a confrontation.

The heavy door closed slowly behind Cali, gradually shrouding the stairwell in darkness. She felt her heart rate rise and instantly regretted her escape route. As embarrassing as it was, she'd managed to reach twelve-and-a-half years of age and she was still scared of the dark. It wasn't just a case of nerves, but a paralysing, throttling, terror-tangling phobia that turned her into a wreck. Cali felt that calling it a phobia made it a perfectly acceptable adult way of saying you were still scared, like a little baby, of something you shouldn't be. Now wasn't the time to worry about whether her fear sounded socially acceptable or not. As Cali's trembling hand reached for the metal handrail, the book slipped out of her bag and fell to the floor. Cali swept the wild, tight curls from her eyes as she knelt down to retrieve it, just as a polished patent-leather Gucci loafer appeared.

Her eyes darted from the shoe to the book before she nervously looked up. Poppy and Martha were standing over her, the light streaming in from behind them, exposing Cali on her hands and knees.

'Ah, Cali, what a lovely surprise to find you here,' exclaimed Poppy, pronouncing every word with more than a tinge of barely-disguised sarcasm. The perfect, doll-like features on her expressionless face didn't match the forced smile on her rose-coloured lips. She stepped on the book, blocking Cali's attempt to tug it away.

'So, what do we have here?' asked Poppy, grabbing the book. Confused, Cali rose to her feet to see Martha grinning, half of her face covered by the latest plus-sized iPhone, held up like some kind of Jedi sword. Its flashlight beamed directly at her, putting her centre stage. The relief at seeing the light was short-lived. Any thoughts Cali had about snatching the book from Poppy were pushed out of her mind as it raced through a number of potential future outcomes; fear flooded her system, making her whole body tremble.

'Focus!' The command seemed to come from outside of her and it was so loud she was sure everyone else had heard it.

'Right, so here we have a very interesting book that's called...' Poppy paused dramatically and spun round, which caused her long blonde hair to swish like she was in a shampoo advert. She faced the camera, ready for the big reveal.

'...*The Rise of the Global Goddess.*' Her blue eyes widened and her fake smile grew. '*The keys to true power and the mystical ways of the witch.*'

Martha began to giggle and the phone in her hand wobbled.

'Well, I'm not even sure what the hell that's all about, but it appears the rumours could be true after all! Cali, it seems, is something of a...now, what would you call it, Martha?' Poppy looked directly into Cali's startled brown eyes. 'Some kind of weird witch?'

'Poppy, I have no idea what rumours you're talking about, and that's not even my book,' said Cali, her voice trembling. How could Poppy have found out already? Cali was angry that her emotions always seemed to betray her. She could feel tears stinging her eye sockets.

'Ooh, Cali, what's wrong? Have you forgotten your spells or something?' The girls laughed loudly.

Cali felt her cheeks flush as a mean voice inside her mind demanded to be heard. *Why are you getting upset? Stand up to her! Say something smart. Do not cry, you stupid girl!*

Cali tried to compose herself. She closed her eyes for what felt like an eternity before gazing back at Poppy. 'It's not my book,' she repeated.

'Ah, no, I'm sure it's not. Let's have a little fun, shall we?' Poppy provoked. 'I think we should have a little read together and let everyone share these special secrets, don't you?' She gave the iPhone a pout and widened her big puppy-like eyes.

'Poppy, please, I don't want any trouble,' Cali mumbled, feeling every last bit of control slip away. A lone tear trickled down her soft, brown cheek.

'Oh, darling,' Poppy exclaimed, 'did we upset you?' Her mocking made Cali feel physically sick and she struggled to swallow. She urged the tear to retract and ordered the floodgates to remain tightly closed. 'It seems that whatever is inside this book is not working very well at all because, well, let's face it, you're a hot mess and a little cry baby! So, let's give our audience, which is basically the entire school and everyone in my incredibly large social media following, an exclusive preview of exactly how we can...erm, activate this incredible power,' Poppy continued with sarcastic delight, posing all the while.

'You have been chosen,' she began, with a dramatic voice. She prodded Cali's chest. 'You are special, and you have the power to heal seven generations back and seven generations forward. By healing yourself, you have the power to heal the world...'

Poppy looked confused for a moment before laughing out loud. 'Seriously, she thinks she's special! Ha, this is hilarious. Power? What power would that be? The power to be incredibly dull or the power to be totally weird? I think a better way to describe you would be more like a pathetic little nobody!'

Cali could see Poppy's mouth moving and the two of them laughing but she no longer registered any sound. The words had already reached deep into every part of her and they were now tearing and stinging like crazy as her insecurities confirmed them all to be true. Cali felt something switch as adrenaline flooded her system. She couldn't believe that, after everything that had happened, she was receiving this same message yet again - only with slightly different words and delivered by someone else: *You're weird, you're an outcast, you're a witch.*

Cali felt an unwelcome yet familiar energy invade her system. It was dark and dense, it strangled and silenced all other options. It prickled and burned as it twisted her insides, scorching cells, as it travelled down from her head and up from her toes, meeting at the centre - at her heart, where she felt an explosion. It felt like it had been gathering intensity over many lifetimes. The pain of not belonging, of being on the outside, of being misunderstood, of never being enough. The fear of revealing who she really was. Some of the pain didn't feel like it belonged to her, yet it hurt her just the same.

Cali felt the force propel her towards Poppy at a frightening speed. She reached desperately for the book but missed her target. Looking down, she saw that her hand was grabbing Poppy's wrist instead. Cali's fingers detected two contrasting pulses racing wildly against each other and she felt a hot energy rise within her again. The force exploded, thrusting Poppy high into the air so that she hovered above the edge of the top step.

For one moment their eyes locked. Cali saw fear in Poppy's eyes. Poppy's feet flapped around in an attempt to find the concrete below. She began to whimper then begged, in total bewilderment, to be set free. Cali observed the scene in slow motion. She felt every element of Poppy's fear and sensed every scattered thought as if they were her own.

'This cannot be happening again,' Cali screamed internally with a ferocity that stunned her.

'I command control of my power,' she said aloud, the vibration of her voice filling the stairwell.

Martha had dropped her iPhone but its flash

continued to illuminate Poppy's flailing figure; it captured her arms waving wildly as she grasped for anything that could save her. The light suddenly increased in intensity, yet it was difficult to determine its source. The whole scene appeared to be encased within a hypnotic, pulsating light. Cali looked at her hands and gasped with doubt and disbelief as she realised it was streaming from her fingertips. At that moment Poppy began to fall.

'Do something!' Martha screamed.

Cali composed herself and the light stream that connected her to Poppy became stronger and solid once more. As she tried to keep her mind focused and her thoughts positive, Poppy's body gradually drew back to safety - the light acting as a lasso, pulling her towards solid ground.

As suddenly as the light appeared, it faded, leaving only the iPhone's intermittent torchlight. Cali felt Poppy's wrist beneath her fingers once again. They stood eye to eye on the edge of the step and, for a brief moment, their relief was reflected back and forth between them in one unblinking stare.

Poppy's expression changed. Her eyes widened, and the colour drained from her cheeks as she yanked her trembling wrist from Cali's grip. 'Let go of me, you freak!' she screamed, as she scrambled for the phone. She smoothed down strands of her hair once she realised Martha was still filming.

'Now everyone will be able to see the witch in action for themselves,' she said as she stared stonily at Cali.

'Poppy, please. I never meant for any of this to happen,' pleaded Cali.

'Save your breath, weirdo. Soon, the whole school is going to know exactly what you are.'

Hungry for Nourishment
Ch 2

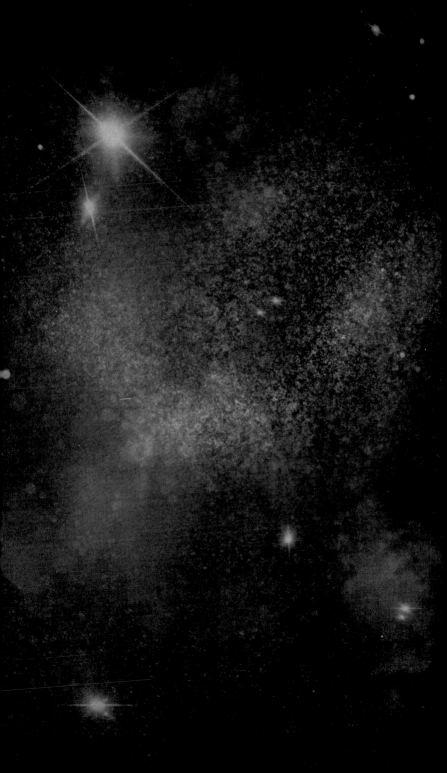

Cali wasn't sure how she managed to get home. Her mum had been 'unavoidably held up'. To say Cali was fuming was an understatement. This whole incident could have been avoided had she been allowed to get the bus in the first place.

The whole journey had been a blur, except for the shock of the nice bus driver asking if she was okay, which set off her waterworks to the point where she felt she might cry a river right there in front of everyone on the jam-packed '172' double-decker bus. She'd hidden the ensuing downpour by shuffling quickly into a tiny spot, squashed between the window and a dusty builder's smelly armpit, so that no one had a chance to glimpse her tsunami-stained face.

Cali's mind replayed the incident a million times. Each time, trying in vain to change the outcome, to stop the encounter, to switch the escape route, to control her power, to not expose herself, to grab the phone and just erase the bloody video evidence. *Why? Why? Why?* Internally, she cursed herself because, no matter how bad things were before, they were about to get a whole lot worse. Cali's mind couldn't be controlled when it came to playing out disaster scenarios, and now it was having a field day. By the time she arrived at her stop, she'd already been expelled from the school, committed to a mental asylum and burnt at the stake.

She grabbed her bag and pushed past the beefy builder, who had fallen asleep standing up and was now snoring out loud. The middle doors of the bus creaked open at a snail's pace; as soon as she could, Cali leaped to the pavement, gasping for air.

She could already see the front window of her home and she scanned it to see if her mum was waiting for her, worried whether Cali would make it home in one piece. She wasn't.

The minute Cali opened the door her senses were hit by familiar smells and the sound of chaos. Even the electronics competed for attention in this house. YouTube was playing, as was the TV and the radio, all of which were drowned out by the barking of Rocco, their cute, strawberry-blonde cockapoo. There was also some not-so-cute, high-pitched singing coming from her little sister's big mouth. Both bounced towards her. The strong stench of damp dog and the pungent aroma of sickly-sweet, perfumed slime overpowered the lemongrass oil her mum diffused, in the hope of banishing such smells.

'Hey, Cali,' squealed her sister, Evangeline, who hugged her legs tightly while wiping whatever stickiness was smeared all over her face onto Cali's black, pleated skirt. 'Guess what happened to me today? Lilly banged into me at playtime and knocked out two of my teeth!'

'Oh, wow, you've lost your baby teeth! Do you want me to get her for you, Eva?' Cali asked, sweeping the crazy mass of afro curls out of her sister's face and pulling a fierce look.

'No, it's okay, she didn't do it on purpose. Plus, it means I get a visit from the tooth fairy and that means I get MONEY!' she shouted, hugging Cali tightly. There were almost five years between them. Cali's mum loved to tell the story of how Cali had wished for a baby sister for years before Eva came along. Only Cali had immediately wished for the baby to go back where she came from, once she'd arrived - something which, her mum explained, was anatomically impossible.

Cali walked down the bare hallway towards the kitchen and wished she could be transported back to her old house - the house that felt like home and which was filled with family photos. Her dad had been out of the country for well over a month, and the change of address only echoed his absence.

Dishes were stacked high on both the dirty and

clean sides of the sink. The breakfast cereals were still on the worktop where Cali had left them that morning. They would never be left like that if Dad was home, but he wasn't due back for a few days yet. The mess was bound to get worse before it got better.

Her mum was perched on a metal stool at the breakfast bar with her coat on. Cali could hear the heavy tapping of her mum's fingers as they moved manically across the keyboard of her laptop. Even though her face was hidden by the screen, Cali knew exactly what expression would be found behind it. Deep lines appeared on her mum's forehead as she stared vacantly into the distance. Cali paused in front of her; she was near enough to smell her mother's perfume but never close enough to be noticed, not that her mum would have stopped what she was doing. Cali felt her stomach sink, like she'd swallowed a heavy stone. She hesitated.

'Hi, Mum,' Cali mumbled to the back of the laptop. 'You'll be glad to see I made it home in one piece.'

'Hey, Cali,' her mum replied without looking up. 'Sorry, I got caught up. I'm under a lot of pressure. How was school?'

How was school?! The compulsory question that came hot off the lips of any annoying parent who isn't remotely interested in what actually happened at school.

'Actually, Mum, it was not good at all,' Cali almost whispered, in the hope that if she said it softly enough, she wouldn't have to acknowledge what happened. 'What's for dinner? I'm starving.'

'Ah. I haven't had time to make anything just yet. Do you want to grab yourself some toast or something?'

Cali could feel her anger rising. Toast? Some bloody toast? If Grandma Gracie had heard that she'd have gone mad. There was always loads of good, tasty food to eat at her house - pots of chicken and rice and peas, ready whenever Cali visited.

'Actually, Mum, I really need to talk to you.'

'Okay, baby, but I have to finish this last bit of work. I've got an important conference call in five minutes. We can do it right after, okay?'

'So you basically asked me a question, but you had no intention of listening to any kind of answer?' Cali was unable to hide her frustration any longer as she peered around the laptop to be face to face with her mum.

Did her mother look paler than usual? Maybe it was just the glow of the screen highlighting the dark circles under her bright blue eyes. Her lips were pursed so tightly that creases had formed and her long brown hair was scraped back with one of Cali's old pink bobbles. It snaked down her back, like Cali's did in the bath when it was wet. That's where their similarity ended. Everyone told Cali that she was the double of her dad. She had his dark-brown deep-set eyes, his flared nostrils and, of course, she'd inherited his black afro hair. Cali secretly wished there was something about her that resembled her mum.

She remembered that, when she was a little girl, she'd 'twiddled' her mother's hair. Apparently, it was a funny family trait passed down from her Uncle Leon. She would twirl the hair round and round her fingers, inhaling her mummy's smell - her favourite perfume mixed with fresh, fruity shampoo. Cali would drape the silky strands across her skin, imagining that the hair was wrapped around her like a cocoon, keeping her safe until she was ready to emerge as a butterfly. Everything was different now. Nobody had time for her anymore, and she worried that her mother didn't want her around at all, after she'd gone through three schools just in the last year under similar circumstances.

'It can't wait. It's something really bad... Mum, it happened again.'

Her mother's fingers froze and she finally looked at

her daughter. 'Exactly what bad thing are you talking about?' Her pale skin turned an even lighter shade and her face hardened. Cali could see that she already knew.

'Oh, no. Cali, you have got to be kidding me. I seriously do not have the time to be dealing with this right now.'

'Mummy's in a bad mood,' Eva piped up as she played with her Barbies in the middle of the floor. Cali watched as her mum held her face in her hands before she slowly dragged her fingers through her hair. Cali, not really knowing what to do, turned to move away. As she did so, her arm caught the corner of a large pink mug. It spilled day-old coffee all over the laptop's keyboard.

'What the hell?!' her mum shouted. She leapt out of her seat as though she'd been electrocuted.

'Mummy, that's a very bad word!' Eva cried.

Her mother shrieked, 'For God's sake, don't you get it? If I don't work, we can't afford to send you to that private school. You're the one who got us into this mess in the first place, by getting yourself expelled. You stupid girl!'

Cali's mum couldn't even look at her. Instead, she frantically shook the laptop and jumped around like a crazy lady. A tug at her trouser leg seemed to jolt her back to reality. She looked down to see Eva's angry face. 'Mummy, you're mean. You're a mean, mean mummy.'

Cali was already in the hallway.

'Cali, I'm sorry. I didn't mean...' She didn't manage to finish her sentence before her phone began to ring relentlessly. Her mum collapsed in a heap on the sofa, any thoughts of going after Cali quickly disappearing. Taking a long and deliberate deep breath, she grabbed the phone, forced a smile onto her face and answered in the most cheerful tone she could muster. 'Hello, this is Corinne Roberts here. Let's get this meeting underway, shall we?'

17

The Invocation
Ch 3

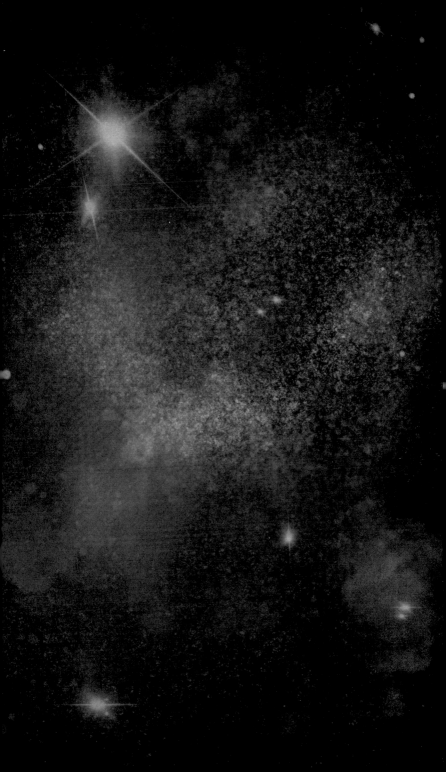

Cali stomped on each stair with enough force to make her soles sting. Her little sister tiptoed cautiously a few steps behind, calling out her name.

'Leave me alone, Eva,' Cali shouted without a backward glance. The tone of her voice caused Eva to turn on her heel; she sat on the bottom step and covered her ears with her hands.

Once inside her bedroom, Cali slammed the door. The mirror on her wall threatened to fall. She held her breath in anticipation of the telling off that would inevitably follow, but no damage was done. She had nothing left within her to hold the mixture of churning emotions she felt. She grabbed her laptop, tucked it under her arm and, with one hand, shakily climbed the white wooden ladder until she reached her top bunk. As she fell onto the bed, huge heart-wrenching sobs spewed up from the pit of her stomach, causing her whole body to retch as they were released into the cold, silent air.

Cali pulled the brown furry throw neatly folded at the end of her bed over her head. The soft fur against her skin felt like a teddy bear hug that she was too big to admit she still needed. She wrapped it tighter around her slender body and peered out from underneath it to look around the room.

When she was five, Cali got the bunk beds she'd always wanted, in a last-ditch attempt to get her out of Mum and Dad's bed to make way for her little sister. Cali was secretly convinced that her mum was scared of the dark, too, as she didn't like to sleep alone when Cali's dad worked away. Before Eva was born, Cali was the one who enjoyed snuggling up to her in that big, comfy bed.

From her horizontal position, nestled amongst her old, well-loved teddies, Cali's blurry eyes scanned the peg board that was full of polaroid pictures featuring happy faces. She barely recognised the girl with glowing, golden skin and sparkling brown eyes, who grinned back at her in her mother's arms. Her hair was plaited, patiently, by her favourite aunt, into neat cornrows. Whenever Cali looked at that photo, she was transported back in time. She could remember every minute detail of that moment - it was only last year. They were on what she'd overheard her mum calling a 'make-or-break holiday'; they'd stayed on a Spanish island and danced outdoors in the hot, humid evening air.

Cali remembered how her mum had pulled her close, how she'd scooped her up into her strong, loving arms and wrapped them tenderly around her, so that Cali's long legs dangled awkwardly around her back. It was probably the last time her mum had held her. They had been so close that their heartbeats seemed to merge as they swayed in time to the soulful music. Cali could still recall the heavy beat of the bass travelling up through her body, vibrating the base of her spine, through each vertebra, and causing the tip of her nose to tingle. In that moment, she realised how the explosion of colour from the sun setting over the deep turquoise sea must have inspired her mum's paintings that hung throughout their old house. The bright colours and angelic wings in many of them made Cali smile and feel like she was never alone when she passed them in the hall. Her mum had painted them when she was much younger, when she'd lived on that same beautiful Spanish island.

'They were created in another lifetime,' was how her mum had put it. Cali could hear her saying how 'the secret to creating was to be still and open, so you could connect to something higher and allow the pictures to float into your imagination and flow through you onto the paper'. In Cali's mind, this conjured up images of angels sending gifts from the clouds, although she didn't think her scrawny stick figures looked like anything the angels would deliver. She made it sound so magical that Cali couldn't understand why she would ever want to stop, but her mum never really answered when Cali asked why she never painted anymore.

Cali vividly remembered seeing the colours swirl around her. Indigo merged with vibrant violet, bright blue blended to green, yellow smudged into orange, reaching out to radiant red. Together, they made a perfect rainbow, and Cali didn't want the moment to end. How sad, she thought, that rainbows always faded so fast...why couldn't they last forever?

Cali pushed back the urge to tear the photo into a hundred pieces. She couldn't stop her mind spewing out a fresh flow of mean, hurtful thoughts that created a confusing mix of emotions and released more tears. She reached for her laptop and opened it up. Instinctively, she began searching. Surfing from YouTube to Netflix to the game centre, but nothing worked. Nothing could take her attention away from the ache within her. The prickly feeling that was so uncomfortable, it made her want to crawl out of her own skin.

A ping from her phone signalled the arrival of a message. She reached out to grab it and looked at the envelope icon that had come from an unrecognisable number. Who could be texting her? Her tummy did a flip at the sight of the unopened message. No, it couldn't be from Poppy, could it? How could she have got her number? Cali hadn't given it to anyone at school. She opened the message, which read:

What a weird little witch and a worthless nobody. Soon, everyone will see the real you.

The threat made her jump, as though Poppy was right there in her bedroom. The intrusion felt unbearable and Cali threw the phone across the bed.

Why did she always attract these mean girls? Why did she never feel like she belonged? Why was she always the outsider?

She arched her spine and flexed her fingers, so that they were spread wide. They hovered above the keyboard. Without any logical thought, the keys formed the words of the question burning deep inside her.

Why am I such a worthless nobody?

Pages of options appeared instantly: a video about how to overcome bullying, an article about recovering from years of self-harm, an interview with a distraught mother whose teen daughter committed suicide. Then there were the usual make-up tutorials to help you mask your issues and look beautiful.

The mouse hovered over the selection of supposed solutions, but none of them spoke to her - because no-one could possibly understand how it felt to be her right now. She sat in a daze, wondering how she could feel so alone when it was possible to connect with the whole world via her laptop. There had to be something or someone out there that could help. Somebody, please.

The words and images on the screen became hazy, then an advert popped up. Cali clicked the small red cross in the corner to shut it down, but as soon as it disappeared, it reappeared - and this time it was flashing. An otherworldly voice fluttered through the speaker, 'You have been chosen.'

Cali turned the volume down and clicked on the cross again to remove the persistent nuisance. As soon as she clicked it, the advert popped back up, repeating the message in the same voice, which made her spine tingle.

'You have been chosen.'

'What on earth is wrong with this stupid machine?' Cali shouted, checking the volume control. Strangely, it was still set to low. 'Please don't tell me it's got some kind of virus.'

She clicked the cross repeatedly, her fingers venting her frustration, but it was no use.

'You are special,' said the voice from the laptop.

'Seriously, I am not special,' Cali yelled at the machine. 'You've got the wrong girl.'

'This is an invitation to join the goddesses. You have been chosen to step into your role as a warrior of the light. You have the power to heal across time and space, seven generations into the past and seven generations into the future.'

Cali froze. It was the second time that day she'd heard those words. She had no idea what they even meant, but they'd definitely caught her attention. She took a closer look at the pop up and saw a group of girls of different shapes and sizes standing together in a circle on top of a high mountain. They smiled, their cloaks flowing behind them like colourful kites on the common. When the camera zoomed in, the graphics were so realistic that it felt as though she could almost touch the purple-tinged clouds floating around their ears. When it zoomed out, she got a magnificent view of a vibrant rainbow land of luscious green rainforests and sparkling, jewel-blue lagoons set against a sunny yellow sky.

'Welcome to The Queendom,' a voice boomed out from the laptop speakers, vibrating through Cali's core. 'Light warriors, are you ready?' the voice commanded. The girls responded in unison.

'WARRIORS! We. Are. Ready. Radiant, inside and out. Ready to shine. Be the light, see the light, speak the light, share the light.'

The girls raised their arms and held hands to connect. Once in this position a flow of light began to cascade into the circle between them. The screen turned dark; only their silhouettes remained. Then, a waterfall of sparkling starlight flowed down from the sky, showering them clean and bright.

'Light Warriors, the world has been waiting for you. Plant your feet deep into the earth and reach your hands towards the heavens. Connect with your sisters in a circle of strength. Together, you're an unstoppable force. You are the children of the universe, here to heal the world. It's time for you to step into your power.'

The light filled their bodies until they glowed from the top of their masked heads to the bottom of their boot-covered toes. Filling and fuelling every cell of their bodies with light, they slowly started to rise - hovering at first, like helium balloons held by string. Then, on release, up they zoom, speeding high into the sky, like shooting stars on their way to the moon.

There was an explosion of colour. A pulsating, hypnotic, cosmic scene with spinning planets and bursting comets all over the screen. A move of the mouse triggered an on-screen motion that made Cali feel like she was on a rollercoaster ride. It was a space-swooping, galaxy-gliding journey, passing planets while shooting further and further into space.

All of Cali's senses were stimulated as something ignited inside of her, pulling her into the game. The concoction was intoxicating and excitement fizzed in her belly like popping candy. She wasn't sure who these girls were, or exactly what they were doing, but Cali wanted, more than anything, to find out.

As suddenly as they'd appeared, the light, the girls and the world were gone and the screen went blank. Cali pressed the spacebar repeatedly and the cosmic backdrop reappeared. She moved her mouse around the screen looking for a way in, but couldn't find anything.

She found herself questioning whether she should really be there. She tried to ignore the familiar feeling of always being on the outside, of never fitting in. Just as she was about to close the laptop, one of the girl's smiling faces filled the screen. She looked a bit older than Cali; she had feathers in her black hair and markings on her face. Little white dots above the line of her eyebrows were in stark contrast to her dark skin. Her striking, green, almond-shaped eyes stared, unblinking, from the screen.

'Maybe you don't feel special right now. You may feel lost and alone, like you don't fit in anywhere. Perhaps you don't believe you can make any kind of difference in the world. That's okay. I felt that way too, before I joined The Queendom. But I want you to know that you're not insignificant, and you're definitely not alone.

'If you've been lucky enough to have received an invitation to join the goddesses, jump on this offer right away. This is so much more than any game you've ever played. You're going to discover powers you never knew you had and you'll finally feel like you belong.

'Being a part of this secret sisterhood has changed my life, and I promise it will change your life, too. You cannot begin to imagine what magical adventures await you. My name is Kai, and I hope to see you on the other side. All you have to do to invoke the Great Goddess is to recite her name three times under the dark moon and click on the key.'

Cali stared at the screen in shock. *How did this girl know exactly how she was feeling?* Her curiosity got the better of her and she clicked on the shape of an ancient key that was spinning on the screen. A wave of regret swept through her, for breaking her mum's rule of never opening these kinds of things. She wondered if it would cost anything, because they really couldn't afford it if it did. As soon as the thought formed in her mind, a response came directly from the advert, easing Cali's nerves.

'Don't worry, there's no charge for this challenge. We need your help. Now say her name three times to open the gateway. Eset, the Queen of Heaven, is waiting to welcome you home.'

Cali looked around the room self-consciously, making doubly sure her door was firmly closed. She whispered 'Eset' three times. She sat, fidgeting, as she waited, half-expecting it to be a prank. The screen remained blank. Nothing happened. Cali cursed herself for being so silly, for believing that she could be someone special.

A subtle, yet strangely familiar aroma reached her nostrils. It was a sweet, floral scent that unlocked a memory of making love potions with rose petals and herbs that she'd carefully gathered from the garden when she was six. The smell lingered in the air without any kind of rational explanation as to where it had come from.

The screen flashed. Symbols and faces appeared, one after the other, in quick succession. Teenage girls, young girls, old women, winged women, warrior women, women wearing crowns, hats, veils; women that were part-animal, part-fish, part-bird, with wings, whiskers, claws, sharp teeth; women adorned with gold; women of every culture, every skin colour, every eye, nose and lip shape; able-bodied women, disabled women...

It was a visual feast of fierce femininity that finally culminated in one woman's face. Her olive skin glowed like a bright, full moon. Her features demanded attention; she had a strong, straight nose pointing to pursed red lips and wide green eyes, lined in heavy black kohl. A gold headdress decorated with ancient script crowned her flowing, dark hair, but it was her enormous wings that made her truly spectacular. The delicate feathers were the colour of emerald jewels and turquoise lagoons, which appeared even brighter against the lava-red sky. A flash of lightning ignited from behind her, sending a stream of light to the sides of the screen, illuminating every corner of Cali's bedroom. The colours reflected

Eset

onto Cali's face, creating a soft, halo-shaped glow that reached the edges of her tight, curly hair. Her belly flipped in excitement, and her big, brown eyes locked hypnotically onto those on screen.

'The invocation of the Great Goddess is complete. She is all that is, was and has ever been. The primal divine feminine force, commander of the cosmos, the greatest power in the whole universe. It is she who ensures the planets revolve around the sun. It is she who makes the wind blow and the oceans flow.'

The words made no sense whatsoever to Cali, but she noticed how they weren't spoken by just one voice, but sung in a melodic chorus. As the vibrations of the sound reached her ears, Cali felt the hair on the back of her arms stand to attention as the skin underneath tightened and tingled. On screen she could now see not just one figure, but a number of beings, which were outlined by a glowing, bright light. Cali couldn't make out the exact details of every face, yet she sensed that they were all women, and as she looked closer, she could see that below their feet wasn't ground, but clouds forming a soft, fluffy floor.

'Welcome to The Queendom. We are only some of the many faces of the goddesses. In time, you will get to meet us all. We are the bridge walkers, the healers, the seers and the witches. We created this game to train light warriors who can integrate the shadow, so that they can find the keys to unlock each energy vortex that will build the rainbow bridge, reconnecting heaven and earth.'

Beams of light shot up around them and above the clouds, projecting out into the dark blue, star-sprinkled galaxy beyond. The beams created shapes with the light and they formed the structure of a magnificent temple, right before Cali's eyes. One of the figures stepped forward into the centre of the circle. Cali realised it was the winged figure whose face she had first seen on screen.

'I am Eset, Goddess of Knowledge and Magic, Queen of the Heavens, the Higher Realm and Upper World. You are hearing this message because you've been chosen for a very special mission.'

A large book appeared in mid-air, right in front of Eset. With a flick of her hand, she scrolled through its thousands of pages until she selected one, then she began to read in a calm yet commanding voice. 'Join forces with the goddesses to restore our rightful place of peace in the world. You are the keeper of the keys who can reconnect heaven and earth. It is time to accept your greatness. You came here at this time to make a difference in the world. Our future is in your hands.'

As Cali stared deeply into Eset's dark eyes, she felt something stir within her that gave her goosebumps. Eset spoke the exact same words she'd read earlier in that book.

'Are you ready to answer the call of the goddess and claim your place as a true warrior of the light? When you enter our world and step onto this path, there will be no turning back...'

Just as suddenly as she'd appeared, Eset's face vanished from the screen, replaced by huge, white marble pillars, adorned with feather carvings, that pointed to a grand gateway. A scroll floated in the centre of the screen. It was labelled 'Your Invitation to enter'. Cali clicked without hesitation. After all, she had nothing to lose.

The Temple
Ch 4

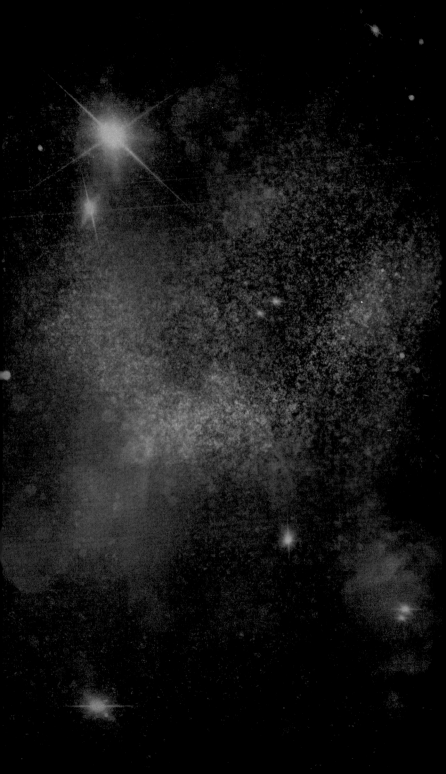

The girl in the advert was right. As soon as the gateway opened, on the other side, was Eset, Queen of the Heavens, waiting for her arrival. Eset sat with a straight spine on a golden throne inscribed with symbols; it was at the end of a large, dark hall that was lit by torches lining the stone walls. Her shimmering white gown swept the floor beneath her and a heavy, gold cape was wrapped around her shoulders. A golden disc, like the sun, crowned her long, dark hair and her glorious turquoise wings were tucked neatly behind her. Two large, regal-looking cats sat on each side of her throne; one with sleek, black skin and the other, the colour of sand. They, too, had wings and were adorned with golden rings through their petite cat noses and pointed feline ears.

'Welcome to the Temple of the Higher Realm. Know that the universe makes no accidents. Everything in your life has led you to this very point.' Eset's voice was deep and commanding. It made Cali feel like she should stand to attention when she spoke, but, being on the top bunk, this was impossible. Instead, she shifted around nervously, making the mattress bounce.

'In The Queendom, you will be called to go within your own soul and unlock the gateways to an unseen world. As a light warrior, you will be able to activate superhuman powers, but this comes with great responsibility. Before you join the sisterhood, we will assess your gifts. We will explore how the planets aligned at your time of birth, calculate your star sign, your numerology and read your palm, to understand your true essence. This will give us the insight we require.'

Cali grew worried. She was concerned that Eset would discover that she didn't actually have any gifts, that she wasn't very special and didn't have what it takes to be any kind of warrior.

'Doubt is your enemy,' Eset answered, as if she could read Cali's mind. 'Everyone is born with gifts that make them unique and everyone has access to greater power, but many have forgotten, and some have chosen not to develop them. Once we embrace our gifts with respect and honour, everything is transformed. Now, answer the questions.'

Cali took a deep breath. Though she could still feel fear and doubt churning in her tummy, she clicked on the book icon. As she selected it, the name appeared: *The Rise of the Global Goddess.*

Cali looked at the screen in disbelief. Was it a coincidence? That was the same book she'd accidentally taken from the library.

'There are no coincidences, only signs and synchronicities. It is how we communicate with you when we have no other option.'

A form appeared on screen and Cali hesitantly entered her name and date of birth. Then a series of statements appeared:

Images often flash in my mind from out of nowhere.
I get strong urges to carry out certain actions.
I can sense how others are feeling.
I often just know things I can't explain.
My dreams are vivid.
I am affected by the moods of others.
I sometimes hear voices and receive messages.

Cali nodded as she read each one and typed an affirmative response. Each question probed things she'd never have admitted to herself, and which she'd tried hard to conceal. She shifted nervously on the bed, wondering if this seemed like a good idea after all. She scanned the rest of the screen for any suspicious-looking elements and peered into the circular camera at the top of her Macbook. Was she being filmed? Was this a set up?

She'd been warned a million times by her parents and teachers about the dangers of the big, bad internet and all the weirdos it contained. How could she trust this was safe?

Eset's face filled the screen and Cali realised she was holding her breath. 'Power only feels like a curse when you don't understand it or know how to control it. It can feel overwhelming, frightening and isolating.'

'What power?' Cali said aloud. Power wasn't something she had much of as a twelve-and-a-half-year-old. Especially not in her world. She was always being told what to do, expected to be a good girl, and she never had a say in anything in her life. Wasn't power something that world leaders or made-up-superheroes fought for? Power seemed to always bring trouble. So, why would she want it? Suddenly, and without warning, her mind flashed to the scene in the stairwell, then it jolted her back to the screen.

A gauge had appeared, with bright green words:

Gift Analysis
Ability to see the unseen - 100%
Ability to know the unknown - 100%
Ability to hear the unheard - 100%
Ability to feel what's unfelt - 100%

Final Result - You are a very rare, highly-evolved, empathic light-being. An empath is a sensitive individual who can read and transform emotion into energy. Instead of having one dominant gift, you have elevated potential to integrate all abilities, in order to connect to higher realms and the unseen world.

Cali read the message carefully three times. She was still struggling to understand what it meant as the next instruction appeared.

'Place your hands on the grid on screen to read your energy and reveal your destiny.'

Cali placed her hands on the outline that appeared. Eset reached out, her hands adorned with golden rings and thick bangles, as if she was touching Cali's hands from the other side of the screen. Her kohl-lined eyes were closed, showing heavy eyelids dusted in metallic gold eyeshadow. Cali instantly felt energy buzzing between her palms and the screen and her hands became hotter. She snatched them away, worried that the laptop was overheating.

'Your purpose is written in the stars, and your destiny marked deep in the lines of your hands. You are a child of the light. Life on Earth must have brought its challenges.'

Cali looked at the screen suspiciously, wondering what the game was really about, and how it seemed so relevant to her.

'They have hidden your power from you so well, that you do not even know it exists,' said Eset, turning her face away from the screen. Cali was sure she saw a tear fall down her cheek. 'Here in the upper realm of The Queendom, we will teach you how to activate the dormant powers within you, to assist with life on Earth. Here, in The Queendom, you are completely safe from harm. No negativity or dark forces can ever enter, for this is a protected, safe space.'

The screen zoomed out and Cali could see a ring of rainbow light surrounding the entire upper realm. 'We are surrounded by an impenetrable sphere of light. But, sadly, this is not the case on Earth. On Earth, you are susceptible to dark forces. Therefore, we need to teach you how to protect your energy and connect to the goddesses, so that we can guide you and keep you safe at all times. Your power could be accidentally activated when you're fearful or overwhelmed by negativity. We also teach you how to face the shadow, by facing it here, in the game, with our guidance and by accessing the lower world.'

The serious expression on Eset's face made Cali stop and pay full attention in a way that no teacher or parent had ever managed before.

'On Earth, you cannot hear, see or feel the goddesses when you are not present. When you are lost in your thoughts. The mind wants to worry about the future or replay past mistakes and pain. Your power is in your presence. You must know, without doubt, that, wherever you are, at any time, and under any circumstance, you're never alone. We're always with you. We're here to offer our guidance, support and unconditional love.

'Let me explain in a way you can understand. When you switch on all your senses you can hear, see, smell, feel and know things that defy all explanation.' Eset clapped her hands and a holographic being appeared on screen. 'This will become your personal avatar here, in The Queendom. It's time for you to experience your first energy ritual. Don't worry, it's as easy as learning the alphabet.'

Cali couldn't imagine that being the case. It was like Eset was speaking a completely new language; however, she was willing to try and understand. 'To connect to the goddesses, to be able to hear our guidance, see the signs we send you, and to feel our love when you are on Earth, you must create a clear channel within you that allows us to communicate. To do this, we activate your awareness, beginning with your breathing - so that you can connect to your heart and higher wisdom. Let me demonstrate.' The avatar on screen suddenly came to life. Its chest expanded and contracted as it began to breathe deeply.

'Take a few deep breaths and allow any thoughts to float through your mind like clouds. Be present in your body and move fully into your heart. This is where we access our power. Let's switch on the senses: hearing, seeing, smelling, feeling and inner knowing.' The ears, nose, fingers, heart, head and belly of the avatar lit up as Eset mentioned each area.

'Now, bring your attention to the crown of your head. See yourself as light encased in a bubble. Send this light up, out of your crown, moving towards the heavens. From this place of peace you ask.'

'What do I ask?' Cali typed into the chatbox.

'Anything, my dear, anything that you want or need in that moment.'

Cali watched as a bubble of light popped out of her avatar's head and hovered there.

'The channel is now open. You are fully connected and your powers can be activated. When you ask for our help, we will be there. You're never alone. It's simply an illusion to believe we're separate. But, remember, it's only in stillness that you will be able to hear us.'

Cali watched the avatar glowing on the screen.

'Now, our second energy ritual for protection.'

A ball of white, glowing light appeared above the head of the avatar.

'Visualise a ball of pure white light just above your head and concentrate on it, so that it grows bigger and brighter. Now, watch, as we bring this ball of beautiful, pure light down, so that it covers your head, neck and shoulders. It moves down to wrap itself around you, until you're encased in the iridescent, powerful light. You must carry out this protection ritual every day, for when you do, nothing can harm you. It repels all negative energy, deflecting it back to the sender. You are divinely protected.

Look between your hands and see the energy.'

Cali saw the pulsing ball of white light appear between her avatar's hands and wished she could see the same thing in real life, however crazy that would be.

'It's energy. Everything in the world is energy. The earth below your feet, the sky above your head. You and your emotions are energy. When you learn how to use it with a clear mind, mixed with the power of intention, you can do miraculous things. Play with it for a moment.'

Cali interacted with her avatar. Moving her hands made the light ball get bigger and brighter or smaller and dimmer.

'Now for the final mantra. It will act as an anchor to expand your light and elevate your energy,' Eset instructed. 'I am safe, I am protected and connected. I am never alone.'

Cali repeated the words softly, in a whisper. The words made her recoil. She was sure the opposite was true.

'You have tremendous power. You have the power to heal - not just yourself, but the world.'

Cali felt tears begin to well as she repeated Eset's words. They felt so alien - enormous and frightening to her, even though it was just a game. Eset didn't know she was just a scared little girl who managed to mess everything up. A girl who was afraid of the dark, who couldn't stand up to bullies, who made her mum mad. She wasn't powerful or special. She was nothing.

The ball of energy vanished from between the hands of her avatar and black and white lines filled the screen as the connection started to break up. Eset's words became difficult to make out. Through tear-stained eyes, Cali could no longer see the images that had brought her so much relief.

'The key to The Queendom will be yours...buzzzz... You have the power to heal seven generations back and seven forward. You are the one to break the cycle...buzzzz...'

Those words sent a shockwave through Cali's body. She tensed as her tears stopped and anger began to rise within her. She thought of her mum, who was too busy to know she existed, and became incensed. She didn't believe any of this rubbish could help her. She slammed the laptop shut.

She was so engrossed that she didn't hear footsteps on the stairs. When she suddenly became aware that someone was outside her bedroom door, she shoved the laptop under her pillow, pulled the bedcovers over her head and turned towards the wall.

'Cali,' her mum said as she stuck her head round the door. Seeing her eldest daughter in bed, she said in a softer tone, 'Are you really asleep so early?'

Cali felt her mum rest her hand beside her and sensed that her face was close. She heard her sigh; she seemed to stand there forever, gently caressing Cali's head, sweeping loose, curly strands out of her face as she leant in to kiss her. 'I'm sorry, Cali. I know I'm not managing things very well at the moment...everything has become so hard. Your dad's away with work so often. I guess I didn't expect to be doing this alone. Sometimes...' She trailed off.

Her voice had a vulnerability Cali didn't recognise. Cali felt guilt rise until it stuck in her throat, threatening to make her gulp. Nothing could have made her move; she was frozen to the core. She needed her mum desperately. She just wanted some attention, yet she hated that this was the case. *Where was her mum when she needed her?* Never there. Forgiveness wasn't an option. She could only rely on herself to work this out.

Head in the Clouds
Ch 5

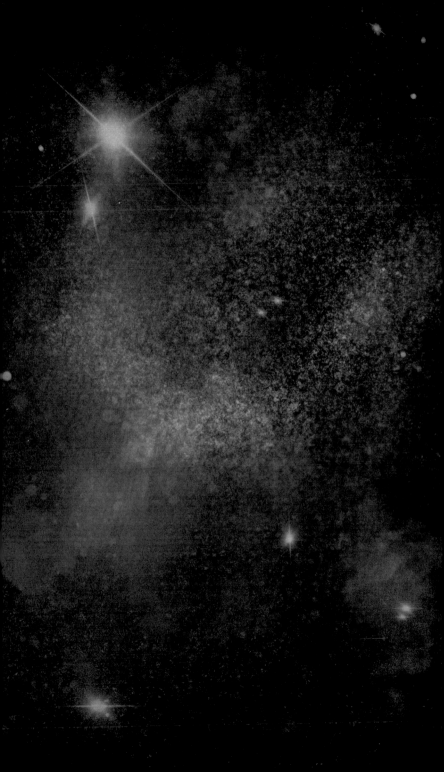

Sat in an old oak tree, Cali watched white cotton-wool clouds roll across the grey sky like they were in a hurry to get somewhere. They were cumulus, the type that created a soft, fluffy floor when you rose above them in an aeroplane. She could feel the rough ridges of the bark digging into her thighs through her black pleated skirt, yet she felt comfortable, high up near the heavens. She held on tightly to a branch and looked down across the field. The old, red stone buildings formed a horseshoe shape around the quaint chapel where they had school assemblies, and were set amongst sprawling green fields as far as the eye could see.

Cali had discovered the oak tree after the worst first week ever at her new school. It was at the far end of the field, past the junior school's chicken coop and compost heap. The smell of chicken poo mixed with leftover rotten vegetables kept everyone else away, but you couldn't smell it if you climbed high enough. It was only two weeks earlier that she'd been paraded in front of the Evans' house group and introduced to her classmates as the new arrival at Crestview School, though it felt like much longer. Some of the girls seemed nice enough, but she supposed her mum was right - these things can take time. Anyway, she liked to take her time when getting to know new people. This was the third new school she'd started in the last six months; Cali was getting used to constant change.

As the new girl, she found that girls would either say all sorts of unbelievable things to try to impress her, or they'd go out of their way to exclude and ignore her. She'd already learned that there were four main cliques in her small house group. There were the polished, pretty and uber-rich girls; the geeky, studious rich girls; the sporty, popular rich girls and the ones that didn't seem very rich or who didn't fit in with any of the others. She didn't like to stereotype people, but the divisions were clear and she knew her place immediately - and that was with the outsiders. No change there, then. She'd thought that things couldn't possibly go any worse than they had at the last school; however, it seemed that she was about to be terribly wrong.

Cali's phone vibrated in her blazer pocket. She reached for it and saw Poppy's name flash up on the screen. Her body tensed.

'Don't miss the special screening I've got planned. I wonder what everyone will say when I expose who the new girl really is?'

Cali felt her whole body flush with fear. It seemed as if the amount of adrenaline running through her veins could shoot her right out of the tree and into space. 'Noooo,' she moaned.

A muffled giggle came out of nowhere, which startled her. She quickly scanned the area below to see if her hiding spot had been discovered. Strangely, there appeared to be no-one around.

'Shush, this is usually the only peace I get,' came a voice.

Before Cali had a chance to properly investigate, she suffered a blunt blow to the head from a scuffed, mud-covered boot. 'Ouch!' she yelled.

After the shock wore off, Cali opened her eyes. She was met by an upside-down face with similar, slightly darker, coffee-coloured skin. The individual's curly hair flowed freely in the breeze and she grinned widely; her chubby, freckled cheeks made her look like a cherub. She had a warm glow about her, which was complimented by dazzling, bright-white teeth, encased by braces. Cali recognised her immediately - it was Zia Ombassu.

'Zia by name, zany by nature,' she remembered someone saying, when Cali had asked who the girl was. Cali had noticed her on her very first day, partly because of her laugh - which was utterly unique and, apparently, something Zia did a lot. Cali also noticed that she was one of the few girls that were just like her. Moving from a multicultural city like London to a sleepy northern village in the middle of nowhere, Cali had gone from feeling totally at home to feeling like the odd one out in every possible way.

'What are you doing here?' asked Cali. 'And why are you upside down?'

'How do you know you're not the one who's upside down?' replied Zia, her trademark cackle following. Cali felt the corners of her mouth begin to twitch. It was probably the loudest, goofiest, most infectious laugh she'd ever heard.

Zia swung her curvy body forwards, so that her hands could grab the branch her knees hung from, and pulled herself to a vertical position. She and Cali were now face to face. 'So, what's up?' she asked, a twinkle in her eye.

'Nothing,' Cali replied, holding her phone close to her chest.

'So you didn't get some kind of horrible message that made you want to throw yourself out of the tree?' Zia responded, kissing her teeth and rolling her eyes to the sky.

The girls looked directly at each other, each with her own sulky, stand-offish stare. Brown eyes locked onto brown eyes. Then Zia pulled the most ridiculous face, which forced Cali to soften and lower her defences. She allowed a little bit of laughter to escape from the corner of her mouth.

'Got you! I can already tell you what your problem is, newbie.' Zia's broad Yorkshire accent made her words feel weirdly warm and welcoming. 'You take everything far too seriously. You need to lighten up, girl!'

'Look who's talking. I'm not the only one sitting up here!'

'Yeah, I guess you got me,' Zia laughed

affectionately. 'I'm just trying to get some peace. Once they start carrying on and falling out over boys, I seriously lose interest and need to escape, quick time. It isn't a boy who's hacked you off, is it? Believe me, they're all total losers.'

Cali felt Zia's eyes scanning her for a reaction. For a split second she thought about telling her the truth. She felt in her gut that she could trust Zia, that she was going to be someone she could hang out with, maybe even depend on. But her head quickly took over and scolded her for being so immature. After all, she'd only just met this girl. What was she thinking?

'No, definitely not,' Cali replied after a long pause. 'I've enough trouble going on without adding boys into the mix.'

'Okay, let me think.' Zia closed her eyes and lifted her head to the sky. 'The text is from a rather popular but unpleasant girl at school and the trouble is with your mum.' She opened her eyes just in time to catch the stunned expression Cali quickly tried to hide.

'Ha! The element of surprise! Never fails. I can also tell by the look on your face that I'm 100% right.'

'How did you do that?' asked Cali. 'You haven't been stalking me or something, have you?'

'Oh, come on, seriously, do I look like some demented stalker?' Zia pulled another funny face that could have seen Cali say yes. But she didn't. 'I get it from my mum. She's really good at reading people. She's like a human lie detector. There's no point attempting to lie to her, as she'll see straight through you in an instant. We're the same, so I guess I'm good at reading people too. I'm not sure, really, this is the first time I've tried, to be honest.'

'That must be a total nightmare, having a mum you can't lie to,' Cali said, relieved that Zia liked talking about herself. It shifted the spotlight away from her.

'I've never thought of it like that. I don't really need to hide anything from my mum. I can tell her everything. She's pretty cool.'

'Everything?' exclaimed Cali. 'Are you serious?'

'Um, yes.' Zia looked confused. 'We're more like friends or sisters, really. I guess because it's just me and her, you see. That's the way it's always been.'

'What happened to your dad?' The words fell out of Cali's mouth before she had a chance to filter them.

'He left when I was three. I don't really see that much of him, to be honest.' Zia read the expression on Cali's face and quickly put her out of her misery. 'I'm actually totally fine about it. My mum is a better person anyway, and I get her all to myself. I might not have a rich daddy who comes to collect me in a fancy car, but we get by just fine.'

'Oh, wow. Sounds very different to my mum, that's for sure,' replied Cali.

'Why's that then?' asked Zia, tilting her head.

'I don't know really. Since we moved, all she does is work - and even when she's not working, she's stressed. Sometimes, I feel like I'm just another thing that gets on her nerves right now.'

'Can't you talk to her?'

'There's no point. I'm pretty much invisible most of the time. She's working so much to pay these ridiculous school fees, which obviously means it's all my fault.'

'What about your dad? Do you get on with him?'

'Yeah, I do, but he works away a lot, so he's not always around.' Cali picked at the bark below her. 'He's got a very important job, saving the world with an international charity. Besides, when he's here, she argues with him. When he's gone, I guess I get it all.'

'That sounds tough. At least you don't have it as bad as some people in the school. I know you think your 'friend' Poppy is pretty awful, but when you see her mum, then it kind of makes sense. She has a big house and a nanny and two swimming pools. She takes six holidays a year and always travels first class, but her mum is a real monster.'

Cali moved around nervously on the branch at the mention of Poppy's name.

'So, my suspicions seem to be right,' Zia said, noting Cali's discomfort. 'You're being lined up as the next victim, one of Poppy's poisonous playthings. I don't usually like to gossip, but on this occasion, I will make an exception. Poppy's mum is even more toxic and obnoxious than she is. She's one of the school governors and she swans around the school like she owns it.'

Zia's eyes were wide and sparkling and Cali found herself wanting to know more.

'Apparently, Poppy's great, great, great grandad founded the school in the dinosaur ages, when it was a lock-in school for boys whose parents really couldn't stand the sight of them, so they shipped them off for weeks on end. Poppy has been at this school forever. Her mum brought her here when she was just nine months old, so you could say she's institutionalised. This school and the people in it are all she's ever known. As you can imagine, she gets bored, and it's only when new prey comes into the school that she has anything exciting to focus on. If they don't meet her standards, she's effective at getting rid of them.' Zia paused and patted Cali's knee. 'I heard there was a girl she took a real dislike to, I don't know why. Anyway, she used to brag that she'd get her out of the school within six months. In the end, the girl's dad's business closed down. He had some kind of nervous breakdown. Poppy was right; she'd predicted the exact week the girl left.'

The colour drained from Cali's face.

'Are you okay?' asked Zia.

'Yeah, I guess so. It's just...I've had a bit of a clash with her. Poppy was being so cruel to that Vanessa girl, so I defended her. Believe me, it didn't go down well.'

'I wouldn't worry too much about Poppy,' Zia said. 'I'll look out for you, and I'm sure she'll lose interest soon enough.'

Cali offered a pitiful smile in return. She wasn't convinced.

'So, are you wondering what everyone else wonders? Go on, you can ask the question,' Zia said, crossing her arms tightly in front of her chest.

'What question?' Cali said defensively.

'The one that everyone thinks of, but is too scared to ask.' Zia paused, unblinking. 'Like, how does my mum afford to send me to this school?' she offered eventually.

Cali looked away, slightly embarrassed. 'I guess I was thinking it, but not in the way you mean. Not in a snobby way. My parents can barely afford to send me to this school, and they never let me hear the end of it. It's like they've finally found a legitimate reason to work even harder and spend even less time with me and make it all my fault.' Cali worried she'd said too much. 'It sounds nice to have a cool mum you enjoy hanging out with.'

'You'll meet her soon, as she teaches history at the school. Mainly to year eight kids. We made some kind of special arrangement for me to come.'

'Oh, wow, that's great,' Cali smiled.

'She also takes a self-study support class after school on Wednesdays, so if you'd like a break from hiding from the poisonous Poppy, you're welcome to join me.'

'Yeah, that would be good.' Cali smiled.

'Maybe, when you realise I'm not just some loud-mouthed crazy girl, you might actually tell me about that text, too.' Zia winked before climbing down. She navigated each branch with the ease of an experienced gymnast and was on the ground in no time. An exaggerated glance confirmed the coast was clear. She waved manically at Cali. 'Laters, newbie.

Maybe see you Wednesday, yeah?'

Cali watched as Zia ran across the field to a group of girls standing near the sports hall. An extra class of history seemed a small price to pay if it provided an escape from Poppy and Martha. A lot of what Zia had said was uncanny. Cali felt she needed to lighten up; it would be difficult to be sad when Zia was around, at least.

Her phone vibrated again. She hesitantly turned it over to see the screen.

'It's showtime.'

Showtime
Ch 6

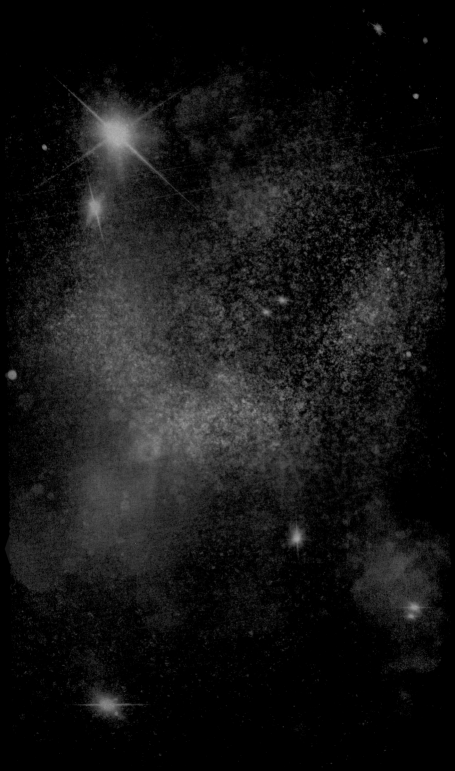

Cali heard shouting and cheering in the corridor - it seemed to come from the classroom she was heading to. It was strange because her science teacher, Mr Early, was synonymous with his name - always ahead of time. He was also very strict.

As she approached, the noise got louder. She peered through the glass panel at the top of the door and saw that most of the class were gathered in a large group at the back of the room. Mr Early was nowhere to be seen. She realised that Poppy was in the middle of the crowd, waving her phone above her head. Cali's heart pounded so loudly, it echoed in her ears. Every part of her was ready to sprint when she felt a hand on her shoulder.

'Running's not going to get you anywhere this time. I've got you.' It was Zia. She practically shoved Cali into the classroom before she had a chance to explain.

'I need you all to shut up and give me some space,' commanded Poppy. She climbed onto a desk to elevate herself above the crowd. It was then she noticed Cali's hesitant entrance.

'Oh my, such perfect timing,' squealed Poppy excitedly. 'Let me present the star of the show.' She held out her arms as though she was welcoming Cali centre stage at her West End debut. The whole class fell silent and stared at Cali.

Cali once again felt an instinct to run. Zia inched closer.

'What on earth are you going on about now, Poppy?' asked Zia, moving in front of Cali. 'Honestly, you're so boring.' She laughed loudly, which made a lot of others laugh, too.

'You obviously got the message, just like everyone else here. So, you must be the teeniest bit interested in getting the lowdown on your new friend,' Poppy retorted, smiling smugly.

'Actually, it looks to me like it's just another 'It's all about me, Poppy show,' smirked Zia. The crowd laughed louder.

'That's where you're wrong, as per usual. Once you see what your witchy little friend did, you'll be laughing on the other side of your face.'

'Yeah, right,' responded Zia, rolling her eyes, which made Poppy's voice rise even higher.

'Let's just say, I don't think your new friend is going to be around for much longer.'

Cali was trembling as she watched the exchange between the two girls play out like a game of ping pong. She could feel the panic rising, clamping tightly around her chest.

'Protect your energy.'

Cali heard the command loud and clear inside her mind and recognised it instantly. Eset was still with her. Just hearing Eset's voice slowed her breathing and eased her fear. But why was she hearing this? Cali remembered that line, the one thing she needed to hear, 'Wherever you are, at any time, and under any circumstance, you're never alone.'

Silently, she prayed that the goddesses would somehow work their magic.

Poppy jumped down from the table and pushed through the crowd to the front of the room. She picked up a remote control and pointed it into the air. A screen descended from the ceiling. Cali felt a stranglehold of fear. She was going to be exposed, ridiculed, outcast...again. Her mind began to race. Then Eset's voice came back, *'Breathe into your heart. Focus on your energy.'*

Cali began to breathe deeply and repeated the affirmation, 'I am safe. I am connected and protected. I am not alone.' She brought her hands closer together and focused her attention on the space between them and sensed an energy ball forming. She looked down and was shocked to see a faintly visible iridescent sphere pulsating between her palms. She panicked for a moment, thinking others could see it too, but no one else seemed to notice.

Cali's eyes fixed on Poppy. She imagined the white ball of energy moving from her hands into Poppy's phone. To her utter astonishment, Cali realised she could see inside the phone in her mind - as if she were holding it in her own hands. Instinctively, she knew exactly what to do. It was as if some mysterious force had bypassed all her doubt, worry and confusion. Her breath became slow and deliberate as her intention became laser focused. She was protected. She would remove the evidence. Like on a movie screen in her mind, Cali could see the phone's screen. She searched through the gallery and located the video, 'her' video. With one swift mental swipe she deleted the video; to be doubly sure it couldn't be accessed, she also emptied the 'bin' for deleted files. The ball of light energy faded then disappeared.

When Cali looked up, Poppy was still waving her phone proudly in the air.

'Right, people, it's showtime! Are you ready to meet the witch?'

Poppy peered down at Cali, her eyes full of a hate Cali could not comprehend. The crowd fell silent. Poppy had their total attention in a way a teacher could only dream of. She swiped up and pressed play. Cali held her breath and closed her eyes tightly. Poppy's pouting face filled the screen. She was sitting cross-legged on a thick, white carpeted floor, deeply engrossed with dressing a large and rather fancy-looking doll. It took everyone a moment to work out what they were seeing, but as soon as they did, the giggling started.

'I have to say that red really isn't your colour, darling,' came Poppy's voice in the video. She had turned the camera back to the doll. 'It makes your skin look ever so drained and a rather terrible shade of pasty pale.' She'd then angrily flung the doll onto a pile of clothes in the corner of the messy room. 'Christine!' she yelled impatiently. 'Where are you? What are you doing?! Christine!'

A response could be heard off screen. 'I'm coming, Poppy, what is it you need? And for the hundredth time, my name isn't Christine, it's Emily.'

All eyes were on Poppy, who was frantically pressing her phone and the remote, trying to clear the screen. Her enormous face flirted with the camera, as she puckered her lips and teased her hair.

'Who did this? Who did this?' Poppy squealed, panic-stricken. She managed to stop the video on a ridiculous freeze frame of her face, cross eyed and pouting. Poppy banged the remote on the desk, in a desperate attempt to make the picture disappear. The laughter and jeering was already at fever pitch.

A boy Cali vaguely recognised from her French lesson laughed loudly and clapped his hands in a slow, deliberate manner. 'Showtime was really spectacular, Poppy! Could not have been better!' The sarcastic grin on his face displayed his perfect white teeth. He gave Cali a cheeky wink when she realised he'd caught her watching him.

'Wow, we really have seen it all now!' exclaimed Zia, whose loud voice could be heard above all the others. 'I knew this would be another episode of the Poppy show, but I didn't realise we'd get to meet one of her favourite dollies.' Zia's signature laugh filled the room.

Cali's eyes turned back to Poppy, who was frantically searching for the missing video. Cali finally relaxed when she recognised, without a doubt, the video was gone. As much as she felt relief, she also felt a pang of sadness. She knew she could never be seen for who she truly was.

Poppy continued flailing. 'No! I have her on video, honestly I do. We caught her using some freaky powers. Tell them, Martha, you saw it too, didn't you?'

Martha stood on the sidelines, speechless. She nodded her head obediently. The jeering continued. 'Whatever, Poppy. Just stop it and sit down.'

The crowd swarmed, laughing and jibing, shoving and swaying like a huge mass of energy, Poppy swallowed up in the middle. Cali saw her struggle to push through to the front. Then they were once again eye to eye, face to face, staring intently at each other but with opposing energies, like the two ends of a battery. Cali felt wobbly inside as the kids became louder and out of control. Poppy glared at her. Cali held her gaze steady; she extended her hand ever so slightly, wondering if she could diffuse the situation. Poppy sensed what the gesture was and recoiled; it seemed to make her even angrier. Her cheeks flushed crimson red. 'I know it's you. You've done something to my phone,' she snarled. 'Don't think for one second that you're getting away with it.'

Just as the words left Poppy's mouth, a deep and commanding voice cut through the madness. 'What on earth is happening here, and where's Mr Early?' A dainty woman with long, dark, braided hair made her presence known. Cali had never seen her before, but she felt a sense of calm the second she stepped in the room. The frenetic energy dissipated and Cali's heartbeat began to slow and soften. There was something familiar about the woman. She turned and saw Zia's face as she sat down at her desk, then realised the connection. It was Zia's mum.

'I don't know what's going on, but it's definitely not what's supposed to be happening here.' Ms Ombassu stood in front of Poppy and held her hand out for the phone. Poppy reluctantly handed it over before strutting back to her chair.

'Where is Mr Early?' Ms Ombassu asked Poppy.

'I think he said something about feeling quite ill,' she replied, wide-eyed and with a look of mock concern.

'Find your seats, everyone, let's get this class into some kind of order. For those of you who don't know me, my name's Ms Ombassu. And we can stop with all this chatter.' She paused as the class reluctantly made their way back to their seats.

'I'm going to take you through a mind-body exercise to help you shift from this state of chaos and regain your focus.' She walked around the class, ushering people into their chairs.

Cali thought Ms Ombassu was the most 'unteacherlike' teacher she'd ever met. She wore leggings and a t-shirt that had a moon on the front. As she passed Cali's desk she gave her a knowing smile. Cali caught a whiff of the deep, musky, floral aroma that surrounded her.

'Now, I want you all to lift your hands high above your heads. Tuck your thumbs into the palms of your hands and make fists.' She perched on the table at the front of the class and demonstrated. 'Come on, hands in the air! Okay, close your eyes. We're going to breathe powerfully through the nose. Inhale and exhale, deep and strong.' The class responded to her direction, even though some of the children peeped through squinted eyes. 'Keep going...in and out, through your nose. You'll all be in great shape in no time.'

This brought some giggling and funny looks, but the class largely did as they were told. Cali took one last peek at Zia's mum and noticed that they had the same soft, slightly-flared nostrils and the same deep brown eyes. As she closed her own eyes, she felt a stab of jealousy; she concentrated on her breathing and the feeling dissolved, replaced by a sense of peace.

'One last deep inhale then hold that breath. Spread your fingers wide and bring your thumbs together so they touch. Now, exhale, lower your hands and open your eyes.'

As Cali did so, she saw Zia grinning at her. She winked, just as Cali's phone vibrated in her pocket. She carefully took it from her pocket and held it under the table so she could view the new message without being spotted.

'Showtime ended up being real fun, don't you think? LOL. Seriously, you NEED to spill all the details TONIGHT.'

Cali smiled back at Zia. Out of the corner of her eye she could see Poppy glaring at her. She felt a strange triangle of energy connecting the three of them, and knew deep down inside that, somehow, the story between them was only just beginning.

When the class ended, Cali hurriedly grabbed her books and rushed out of the classroom. She'd had enough drama for one day and wanted to get away, fast. Without looking up, as she went to push the outer door of the school, she instead bumped straight into the boy from earlier. He was much taller than Cali and her hand awkwardly collided with his chest. She dropped her books in her shock then kneeled to retrieve them. He did the same. Cali hesitantly looked up and met his gaze; she hoped he wouldn't notice that her cheeks were flushed.

'Hi, I'm Nate.' He had a crisp American accent that instantly made him sound both confident and interesting.

'I'm, erm...'

'Cali. I know. Poppy already introduced you.' He grinned as he handed her a few of her books. 'Well, see you around.'

He stood and walked away. Cali had to catch her breath. It took a minute, then she rushed off in the opposite direction.

The Car Ride
Ch 7

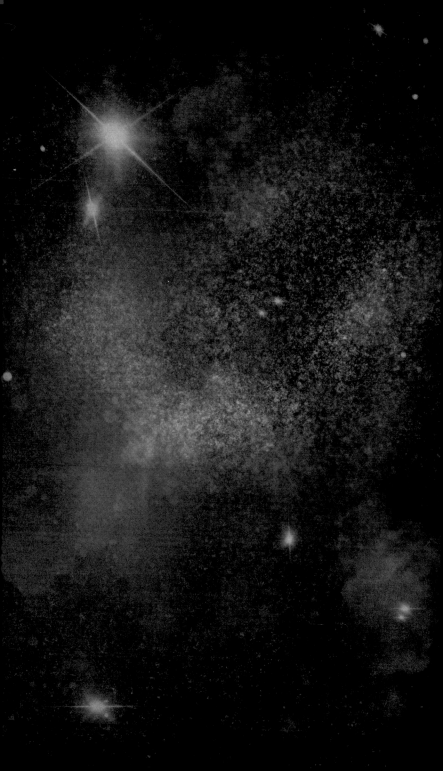

Cali pressed redial on her phone for the third time. The rain lashed against her legs, which made her tights stick to her like an itchy, soggy second skin. She angrily muted the automated message. 'Muuuum!' she muttered sulkily into the phone. 'Where are you?'

School now finished for the day, there were only two other people left in the car park. She didn't know either of them. She'd watched as the kids from all the after-school clubs and classes had been promptly collected - and there she remained, waiting for her mum to pick her up. Yet again.

Cali looked up to see her mum's black Range Rover screech into the tree-lined school driveway. As Cali approached the car she could hear her mum's 'posh work voice'. She was relieved that nobody else was there to hear it.

Cali moved a stack of papers from the dirty front seat and climbed in. She stared at her mum, looking for some kind of acknowledgement, and received a raised eyebrow, which must have meant 'hello'.

Cali felt as if she could burst. The drama had happened during the last period, and Zia had left with her mum. Cali had felt completely alone. Her head was filled with noisy thoughts, all vying for her attention; it was hard to make sense of any of them. At least now the video had gone, she wouldn't get into trouble with her mum. Maybe she'd even get a little empathy.

She waved and mouthed the word 'Mum' with an expression of urgency. Her mum shook her head and continued talking to her colleagues. Cali felt her energy deflate like a popped balloon and angrily plugged in her earpods. She turned up the music to drown out the annoying work conversation that was being broadcast through the car's internal speakers.

After some time, a hand on her knee brought her

out of her daydreaming and back into the car. 'Sorry, Cal,' her mum said, in a forced cheery tone as she tried to catch her eye. 'I had to take that call. We're so behind on this deadline, it's all going crazy. How was school today?'

The obligatory daily question was shoved at the end of the sentence like an automatic afterthought. Cali wondered if she should share anything, but she needed to shed the emotional weight she'd been carrying.

Her mum sucked on a vape pen and blew clouds of vapour out of the car window. 'Oh, it's like that, is it?' she said. 'Too cool to speak to your old mum now, eh? What do I have to bribe you with to get a conversation these days? A McDonalds? A movie? That new top you had your eye on?' She pouted and gave a look of mock rejection.

'Maybe just paying a bit of attention would go a long way,' Cali answered.

'Ouch! That hurt. You know how hard I have to work now, Cali. Come on, be fair. You're the whole reason I'm doing this. I'm going for this promotion for you, to keep you in that bloody school.'

'I knew it would be my fault,' muttered Cali.

'Well, technically speaking, it kind of is, Cali, isn't it? Who was it that got expelled?'

Cali felt her throat tighten as her mum's words stung. 'You might not want to hear how school went today, in that case,' she snapped.

'What does that mean? I suppose you could always wait until your dad's back home at the weekend and speak to him about it, if you wanted.' Her mother turned her attention back to the road. They both knew school was something she could never speak to her dad about. He was super strict and very protective. He sometimes lost his temper over the slightest slip in grades.

'Mum, I'm going to tell you.' Cali took a deep

breath. 'Because I need you to listen. There's been another incident.' She sat back, a little shocked that she'd said it and feeling the enormity of her words. They hung in the air; it felt almost suffocating within the confines of the car.

'What exactly do you mean, Cali?'

She could physically feel her mum's tension. 'I tried to tell you yesterday, but it's never the right time, is it?'

'Well, I'm all ears now. Tell me what's happened.'

'The thing, you know...' Cali hesitated.

'You're scaring me. It's not the thing I think...'

'Yes, that thing. My powers, my abilities, whatever you want to call them...they came out again. It was almost the same as last time. These girls were following me and making fun of me, and then, before I knew it, we were on the stairs. The other girl, she fell...or I made her fall, I'm not really sure. It all happened so fast. Then I managed to bring her back, and the light came, then I realised they were filming and it was too late...' Cali could feel her heart pounding in her throat. She avoided her mum's gaze until she'd finished. When she looked up, she could see her panic reflected back.

Her mum pulled over at the side of the road and the car came to a halt. She turned to look at Cali. 'You're telling me that this thing happened again? How on earth could it have happened again? And there's a video? A video, Cali? Do you understand how serious this is?'

'Hang on, I haven't finished yet. It's okay, really it is. I deleted the video. It's gone.'

'What?' Her mum looked confused. 'How, Cali? How exactly?' As she studied Cali's face, it was like she could read her daughter's mind and answer her own question. 'Wait a minute, I know, with the same powers. Is that how you removed it?'

'Yes, Mum. I found this game last night...or rather,

it found me. I think it's got something important in it that I need. It taught me how to use the energy in a different way, then today, in class, I got to use it. Poppy was about to show the entire class the video on her phone, and I was so scared, but I just focused. Then I could see inside the phone and I was able to delete it. It all happened with just the power of my mind. Somehow, I was able to transform the energy.'

'Back up now. You're acting like this is a good thing. We've spoken about this exact topic many times. No good will come from any of this. Listen to me. I know this for a fact.'

Cali noticed her mum was shaking. 'You weren't there. Seriously, it was actually kind of cool. I think I'm starting to learn how to control it.'

'Don't be deceived. You're not in control here. You cannot let this out. You must suppress it. If you ignore it, it will go away.'

Tears streamed down her mother's face. Cali felt a mixture of confusion and fear cloud her mind. She didn't understand why her mum was overreacting, though it was exactly what she did last time. She'd just wanted to shut the whole thing down without any discussion.

'But, Mum, it won't just go away. You don't understand what it's like.'

'It's common sense. With these sorts of unwelcome experiences, you just have to shut it down. If you feed it, it will get stronger.'

'How can you know that?'

Her mum reached for Cali's hands. 'Cali, listen to me, no good will come from this, it never has. It's not something you can control. You have to promise me...'

Cali resisted the urge to pull her hands away. 'Promise you what? The same stupid promise I made when I was a little girl?' She looked up to see her mum staring at her intently whilst nervously biting the edge of her lip. She looked like a hurt little girl herself.

Her mum pulled her hands away and started the car. 'This is non-negotiable. I will not be wasting another second of my time dealing with your crap.' Her tone was sinister and Cali felt a sting, as if she'd physically slapped her. The shock instantly produced fat tears; she turned angrily to look out of the window to ensure they stayed hidden.

'If I were you, I wouldn't mention a single word of this to your dad. He'll be back tomorrow, and if he even gets a whiff of any trouble at this school, I dread to think how he'll react.'

Cali silently watched raindrops race down the window and wondered if her tears would be able to beat them. In her head, she had a smart response that would make her mum think twice about being so mean and hurtful. But, in real life, she felt an ache in her heart that choked her into submission. She swore to herself that she would never keep the stupid promise. Her mum wasn't capable of keeping any of her promises lately, so why on earth should she?

The Queendom
Ch 8

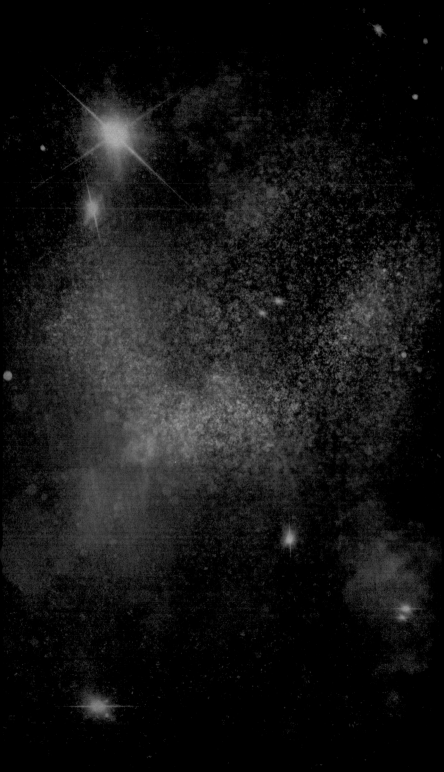

Their journey continued in an awkward silence. Cali burst out of the car door before the engine had even stopped; the heavy atmosphere had created a pressure that propelled her out the minute she could escape. The rain was a welcome relief, almost as if it was able to wash away the sticky residue of whatever her mum had projected onto her.

Cali didn't look back as she slammed the car door behind her. Once inside, she ran straight to her room, discarding her coat halfway up the stairs and kicking off her shoes. They rebounded off the wall, leaving black marks on the white paint.

The bunk beds that had once seemed magical to Cali, allowing her to sleep nearer the stars, now felt like a hassle every time she climbed the little wooden ladder. She wished she could transport herself straight into bed without having to lift her heavy legs and find the last bit of energy she had to haul herself near the ceiling. Once up there, in her safe place, memories of the day came flooding back. It was a concoction of extreme highs and lows, fear and frustration, sprinkled with utter confusion. As scenes replayed on the movie screen inside her mind, she felt frustration angrily stamping its way up her chest, demanding to be let out, but it felt too frightening to do so.

Cali switched on her TV and flicked through the channels. She stopped on Disney, and American accents filled the room. A group of pretty girls with dazzling white teeth and long, shiny hair were laughing. They always said the right thing at the right time, confident and clear. Cali wondered why she always felt like the odd one out. Maybe she just wasn't good enough or smart enough to be one of those girls. They made it look so easy. Their laughter began to ring in her head, taunting her, reminding her of all the times in her last school she'd been told she wasn't welcome; all the times her so-called friends failed to stand up for her; how she always seemed to attract girls who made her feel bad about herself. Cali had no way of turning off her thoughts and silencing the girls in her head, but she could at least silence the ones on screen. She pressed the off button and flung the remote control across the room.

Her phone beeped persistently as messages arrived in quick succession. Cali grabbed it to look at the previews. Despite there being a whole screen full of messages from Zia, her focus was drawn to the one name that had managed to force its way into her inbox. Even the sight of it made Cali's stomach flip, and it threatened to expel her lunch.

POPPY. POPPY. POPPY.

Cali felt her breathing become faster as she looked at the closed message envelopes. She wished she had the strength to delete each one and block Poppy completely. But she couldn't ignore them; they taunted her, demanding to be read.

> *'Don't think you've got away with this, you witch.'*
> *'You're a worthless nobody. Soon, everyone will know what you are.'*

That word. That stupid word. **Witch.** She was not a bloody witch! It followed her, and no matter how far she ran from it, it always managed to catch up to her.

Does not following the crowd automatically make you a witch somehow? Cali couldn't understand why she was always the weirdo, the misfit, the outsider. Why did she have to change schools and start all over again? What was it about her that made her a magnet for mean girls? Cali didn't get why they had to be that way. Why she wasn't brave enough to stand up to them. To confront them, to stop them...to be able to control these stupid tears.

She grabbed the big furry bear sitting next to her and delivered a blow to its overstuffed belly. She wished it didn't have to be this way.

Another beep on her phone. She grabbed it to see a message from The Queendom.

Cali stared with disbelief. Even the game was texting her now. Part of her wanted to ignore it, but another, more desperate, part of her thought this may be her only hope. If it wasn't for what Eset had shown her, things could have ended disastrously at school. It was becoming clear that she couldn't rely on her mum for anything, least of all her issues with Poppy. But she was learning that she wasn't alone. She was through with doing what she was told, so she opened the message.

Come explore The Queendom...
Your avatar awaits...
Create your unique light warrior...
Join me in the Star Chamber...
Eternally, Eset x

Cali slouched back into the soft pillows supporting her and clicked on the link; it brought her directly into the game from her phone. As it opened up, she was met by the dreamy blue, red and purple cosmic skyscape. There was a weird key spinning around in the centre. It was like a symbol, a cross with a loop at the top, and the words '*The Queendom*' filling the screen.

'I see you, soul star sister. I want you to know that you're special and unique.'

Cali recognised Kai, the girl from the advert; she appeared with a message for her.

'Do you want to know how it feels to have the confidence to truly love who you are? To have the freedom to be yourself and not be affected by what others think? To feel protected, supported and

connected? To be part of a secret sisterhood? Then you're in exactly the right place at exactly the right time.'

'Be the light, protect the light, share the light!'

'First, select your avatar, explore The Queendom and get ready for your first mission. Then you'll be able to join us, and together, we will learn the ways of the light warrior.'

Cali felt inspired by the promises, even if it seemed like she would never be a part of anything; she had to believe it was at least a possibility. She clicked on the strange looking key that was spinning around the screen to enter.

The main menu on screen showed an electronic version of an ancient map, with hand-drawn illustrations of all the different locations in the game. Each place lit up in fluorescent pink when hovered over. There were three different realms in the game, and Cali was in the higher celestial realm.

Map of the Queendom

Celestial realm - Upper World (Star Chamber, the Light Temple, the ascended masters' Nerve Centre)

Earthly realm - Middle World (the great Tree of Life at the axis of the worlds)

Shadow realm - Lower World (the Garden of Eden, the cave of the lost children, the crystalline core - centre of the Earth)

The illustration showed that the whole of the Queendom was surrounded by a sphere of rainbow light, like it was encapsulated in an impenetrable, protective bubble. Within it was the Light Temple, the Nerve Centre and the Star Chamber.

'Proceed to the Star Chamber to create your avatar,' the game commanded.

Cali spotted the Star Chamber on screen. It was a huge pyramid structure made of gold. As she clicked

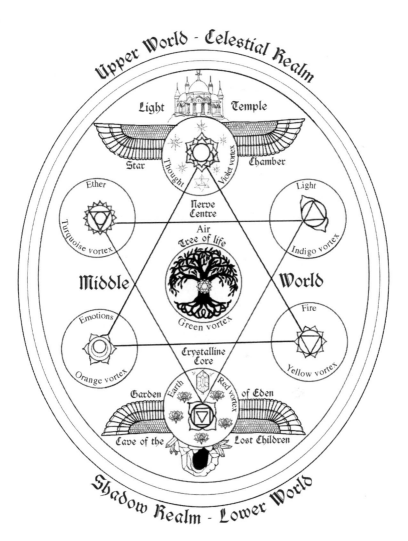

Upper World - Celestial Realm

Light   Temple

Star   Chamber

Thought   Violet vortex

Nerve
Centre

Ether   Light

Turquoise vortex   Indigo vortex

Air
Tree of life

Middle   World

Green vortex

Emotions   Fire

Orange vortex   Yellow vortex

Crystalline
Core

Garden   Earth   Red vortex   of Eden

Cave of the   Lost Children

Shadow Realm - Lower World

The Queendom

on it, she could see that its walls were formed of stars, as if it just floated high in the cosmos. Once inside, an electronic catalogue was displayed, where Cali could choose elements of her avatar. The graphics were hyper-real and on display were endless variations of body shapes, skin shades, hair styles - even lips and nose shapes and eye colour. Cali loved these types of games.

The first thing she did was to make her avatar much taller than she could ever realise, genetically. She added strong thighs and muscular arms, which were in stark contrast to real-life limbs, which were gangly, had too much hair and bruised easily. Cali chose the hair she'd always wanted: long, dark and straight, reaching all the way down her back to tickle her waist; the kind of hair that swirls when you turn around, rather than big and bushy. She selected the same sun-kissed skin tone as hers, just so that some element of her remained, but she added a sprinkle of freckles and made her eyes bright blue, like her mum's. When she'd finished selecting the various elements, she looked proudly at her avatar-self on screen. She raised her hands high above her head, in the same pose she'd seen the others create. She finally looked like a real light warrior.

Eset's striking face filled the screen. Heavy gold jewellery adorned her elegant neck, stacking up towards her angular jawline. 'Welcome, beloved, you look simply divine. Your work in the Star Chamber is almost complete. I see you've focused on the outer physical qualities, but there is deeper beauty to be found within, and so much more that makes up a true warrior of the light.'

Cali worried that she'd made a mistake or failed some kind of test. She moved her avatar to the centre of the Star Chamber, under the tip of the pyramid. She watched as a bright star moved into place above her avatar's head.

'This is Sirius, the brightest star in the universe. When it comes into this particular alignment, it creates a powerful portal of energy. Stay below it, let us activate the real qualities of your soul. Your true beauty can only ever come from within.'

Cali watched the light come through the crown of her avatar's head. It streamed down the centre of its body into two snake-like channels. When it reached the base of its spine it lit up a red sphere, and the words *'I am safe'* appeared in luminous writing. The snake light channel moved up slightly, to just below her avatar's belly button, lighting up an orange sphere and activating the words *'I am creative'*. Just above this, a yellow sphere glowed as bright as the sun, signalling the words *'I am powerful'*. Then the light travelled to its heart, where a bright green light was emitted, together with the words *'I am loving and kind'*. The snakes moved up to the throat, which turned blue and spoke the words aloud, *'I speak my truth.'* Next, an eye appeared on her avatar, right between its eyebrows, as did the words *'I see the unseen'*. The light snaked out through the top of the avatar's head, where a golden crown sat; there, the words *'I am connected and guided. I am not alone'* appeared. Finally, the light sparked a vortex above the head, which opened like the petals on a flower.

Her avatar stood before her, with a line of circular spinning wheels, lit up like the colours of the rainbow. Cali looked in amazement at the bright, glowing figure on screen. Eset clapped her hands and the stream of light ceased.

'You are the keeper of the keys.' She smiled at the glowing figure. 'The purpose of this game is to complete the challenges in each of the seven realms. Once you find the key to open the vortex within, the seven spinning light spheres that you see here on screen will create a rainbow bridge connecting heaven and earth, in order to restore The Queendom to its former glory.'

Eset paused, and in that moment, Cali felt like she could dive into the dark pools that were her eyes; she was sure she would never reach the bottom. 'To win in this game and succeed in your mission is as much an inner journey as an outer one. You will need to face your fears, meet your inner demons and step into your true power if you're to overcome the challenges you will be faced with. There are dark forces at work in the world. They've tried for centuries to silence our stories. We've been portrayed as witches, seen as evil; we've been hunted, tortured and banished from history as myths.'

Cali felt her spine stiffen when the word *witch* was mentioned. But as Eset spoke an illustrated story appeared on screen that showed a woman being dragged from her house screaming. Her head was covered and her wrists bound. She was burnt at the stake in front of a jeering crowd.

'These forces have sought to strip us of our power, dismiss our abilities, paint us as monsters and turn us against each other. In doing this, they've affected all the women of the world. It can be difficult to understand because they've hidden your power from you so well that even you do not know it exists. Here, in The Queendom, you will begin the process of unlearning the lies you have been taught whilst returning to your true power.'

'What about joining my tribe?' Cali typed into the chat box at the bottom of the screen 'When will I meet them?'

'You will meet your soul sisters soon, but your first mission must be completed alone. We are relying on you to spread the light of the warrior throughout the world, so that it shines so bright it can never be denied again.' As Eset said this the light on screen grew in intensity. It got brighter and brighter until her face vanished and Cali could only hear her voice: '*Join me in the Light Temple. It's time for your initiation.*'

The Initiation
Ch 9

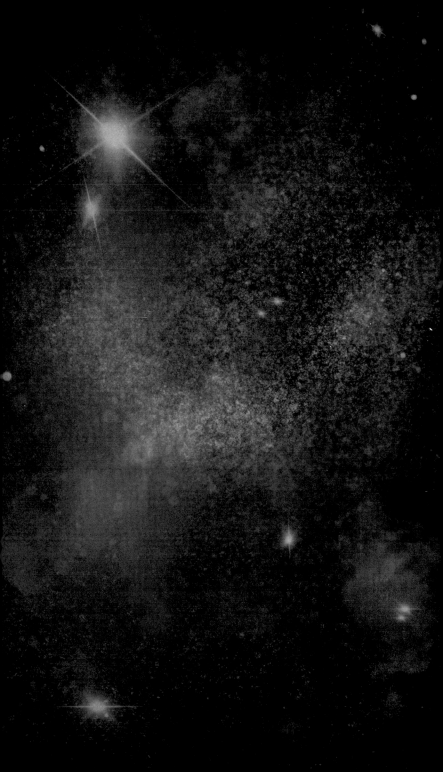

𝐂ali watched as the constellations of stars and planets and galaxies danced and swirled around her. She was mesmerised by the astral paint palette. The sky was filled with beautiful, bright tones of blues, pinks, purples and yellows, which merged together on the dark blue backdrop sparkling with starlight. The Light Temple came into view below her. Beams of ultraviolet light created a glowing outline of the magnificent structure that sat proudly on purple-tinged clouds. Cali's avatar landed on the entrance steps and glided past the four huge pillars of light that framed them. It was surrounded by vines made of asteroids and light-filled lagoons whose waterfalls spilled shining stars. The majesty of the temple took her breath away.

Once inside, the temple looked like an ancient stone building with exotic flowers adorning the walls. The goddesses she'd seen at the start of the game floated down the corridor, gesturing for her to follow. They arrived in a grand hall where Eset sat regally upon a golden throne with her two giant cats on each armrest. Electric-blue serpents entwined her winged arms, and in her hand she held a wand that had a lotus flower blooming from it. Her long, dark hair and golden gown flowed behind her, and her magnificent wings filled the space.

'The light in me honours the light in you.' Eset smiled gently, bowing her head. 'You will soon come to remember your true self. You are a being of light. You are a child of the cosmos, and the cosmos is within you. The same atoms in your body were forged inside stars. Just like them, you were born to shine your light.'

Not everything Eset said made sense to Cali yet, but the words felt good in her body, especially in her heart. She liked the sound of being a child of the cosmos, a sister of the stars. It felt like she was part of something, a big, beautiful, never-ending mystery. Eset stood up and, as she walked, her heavy cloak trailed on the stone floor behind her. As she touched the top of Cali's avatar's head, a stream of light poured out from Eset's hands, down her avatar.

'You will soon come to understand just how important our light work is in the world. Without it, dark forces will succeed in destroying your planet. To create peace and balance in the outside world, we must first create it within us. When we heal ourselves, we heal the world.'

As Eset spoke, she held out her hands. Cali watched as the energy ball appeared then transformed into shapes that represented the words she spoke. A play of forces, of both the light and the dark, cast a shadow across the globe she held in her hands.

'It's time for your initiation into The Queendom. This is an inner journey that can only be taken alone. Before your first mission, I need to tell you two important things. The first is the ankh that you will be looking for.'

As Eset said this word, the ancient key shaped like a looped cross that Cali had seen at the start of the game appeared between her slender palms. 'The ankh is the sacred key to the cosmos, and it unlocks mystical powers. It's a powerful healing crystal that will give you courage, strength and access to this realm. It's your mission to find all seven of them, to unlock the inner and outer gateways that will rebuild the rainbow bridge. Each ankh contains a different coloured crystal that represents each of the seven realms. When you are 'in flow' and connected to all things, we begin to co-create with the universe. Where focus goes, our energy flows, and we can conjure up objects. This key is an example. You may never have seen a key like it before, but now you need to find it; suddenly, it will appear. These are signs that you are on the right path. We will send them to you. Trust them.'

Various ancient ankhs appeared in quick succession; they spun in front of her avatar's face, each one bearing a rainbow-coloured crystal at its centre.

'The second thing you need to know is about the shadow. We're all made of both light and dark, and we must embrace both parts.' Eset brought her hands together in a prayer at her heart. The energy between her palms shone out in streams of light. 'The shadow exists within all of us. In your first mission, you will come face to face with the Dark Goddess. Here, in The Queendom, we're able to guide you as you face your inner demons; we accompany you to the underworld to do this.'

'*What are inner demons?*' typed Cali, wondering whether she actually wanted to know.

'Demons that are found in your head. The ones that tell you that you're not smart enough, pretty enough or good enough. They may whisper or shout or keep you awake at night. They compare, judge, doubt and criticise you, like an inner bully.'

Eset removed her heavy velvet cloak and wrapped it around the shoulders of Cali's avatar, pulling the big, soft hood up over its head and taking its face in both hands. She looked into the avatar's eyes and said, 'It's time. You're ready for your first mission. Follow the red thread, it will lead you to the underworld. But beware, the gateway is guarded by the Dark Goddess. You will have to face her if you are to reach the garden and collect your first key.'

Eset returned to her throne and Cali's avatar stood before her. 'These are my daughters - Sekhmet, the Warrior Goddess, and Bast, the Goddess of Protection. Bast will accompany you on your first mission.' Eset reached out her hands and stroked her cats' heads. They purred and stretched at her touch.

'Bast, darling, to the lower realm.' Eset signalled to

the black cat, who stared straight into the camera with its piercing yellow eyes. The cat stood proudly, then it spread its jade-coloured wings and lunged forward as though it might leap right out of the screen.

The screen then displayed the digital map, with its glowing pink illustrations of the three worlds. In the centre of the map was a beautiful painting of the Tree of Life. Cali studied how it was planted in the middle world, but connected to the upper world by its branches, which reached towards the stars. Its roots dug deep into the lower world. Cali didn't have time to take it all in before the sleek, black, flying cat landed gracefully before her.

'Hey, girl, I'm Bast, daughter of Eset, as you know. Oh my, oh my. Please forgive me, but wow, it's just so exciting to meet you. I can feel your energy so strongly already, and you haven't even unlocked your first vortex yet!' The cat purred and rubbed her dark, glossy body against Cali's avatar. She then arched her back and stretched out her paws.

Cali watched the huge cat curiously. She was the size of a tiger yet as graceful as a housecat. She spoke in a fast but friendly voice.

'You can type any questions you have into the chat box and I'll answer as we go. In fact, I'll start with the question everyone asks, and that's why our game is called *The Queendom*.' Cali nodded in agreement at the screen, relieved she wouldn't have to ask something so apparently obvious. 'The Queendom is a world run entirely by women who honour Mother Earth and the cycles of nature. This is a good thing, because, in your world, there's quite a lot of chaos. I mean world poverty, global warming, animal extinction, corruption, wars...do I need to go on?'

Bast took a deep breath and pulled a funny face, which made Cali smile. The cat shook her head. 'Yeah, so we need to, like, fix that before we can get to anything remotely resembling an equal balance. Make sense?' Cali nodded in agreement. 'Anyway, I digress. Let me give you the lowdown. There are three realms, or worlds, in The Queendom: the celestial realm that is the higher world you've already accessed; the middle world, which you know as your planet Earth; and the lower realm, or underworld, where you get to face not only the Dark Goddess, but also the shadow parts of yourself you'd rather pretend didn't exist.' She smiled, her long whiskers twitching. 'Jump on my back, let's travel through the Tree of Life. That's the only way we can descend.'

Cali instructed her avatar to straddle the cat's back, and together they flew through the cosmos, swooping and gliding their way through the clouds until they could see the middle realm below. They landed in a grassy field, beneath a bright yellow sun, next to a huge oak tree.

As soon as Cali hopped off Bast, the sleek cat folded away her wings and changed into her female goddess form. Bast was a beautiful, young, slender woman with dark skin and shiny dark hair, just like Eset's; she had the most striking cat-shaped yellow eyes. She wore a long, jewelled skirt and gold bangles were stacked around her neck and wrists.

'You can bow before me now. You're in the presence of a goddess, don't you know?'

Cali quickly made her avatar bow, then saw Bast laughing.

'Oh my goddess! I'm just joking. I thought it might be nice for us to meet, girl to girl, before we descend. Most goddesses can shapeshift, you know.' She winked.

They stood together before the sacred oak tree. Cali toggled her view to the branches above her, which travelled all the way to the stars.

'Seriously now, we're standing before the great, wise Tree of Life, which is in the centre of the three worlds. It's actually an energetic doorway that leads above and below, allowing you to journey to the underworld. Its ancient roots reach down into the depths of Mother Earth's womb, to the crystalline core, at the very centre of the earth, where the giant ruby heart can be found.'

'What is in the underworld? It sounds kind of scary,' Cali typed into the chat box.

'Well, it's not all scary exactly. You'll find the most beautiful garden you could ever imagine, the Garden of Eden. But you'll also find the cave of the lost children in the Valley of the Shadows. Anyway, we don't need to talk about that right now.' Bast looked away. 'This first mission is all about getting familiar with your dark side. Remember, you need to gather the red key. So, all you have to do is approach the guardian of the gateway and ask her for the key.'

'That's all?' typed Cali.

'Yeah, that's kind of all,' answered Bast, giggling nervously. She twitched her nose, just as she did when she was in cat form. 'The Dark Goddess is a true reflection of your shadow. So, whatever you're trying to hide, deny or avoid will be right there in your face.'

Cali felt a little nervous from all the talk of darkness and shadows. Even if it was just a game, it felt like things were becoming a little sinister. *'What if I'm not quite ready to do the mission?'* she typed.

'Oh, girl, nerves are normal, trust me. But don't let doubt stop you. You're ready. You were born for this.' Bast reached out and hugged Cali's avatar, which made it glow a little brighter.

'Now, before we approach the tree, reach out to touch the bark. To proceed, we must pause, breathe, and ask permission. If the spirit of the tree allows you to enter, we give thanks and pay our respects to the cultures and ancient tribes who have shown us the way by sharing their teachings. Then we say a prayer for protection.'

Cali moved her avatar so it reached out to touch

the tree. A red light spread from its fingertips into the trunk and down through the roots into the earth. She saw the red light like a thread travelling downwards through rich, moist soil; down, past pebbles and stones, through the earth's layers, through water, until the screen went completely blank.

The beat of a drum, slow and steady, like a deep, resounding heartbeat, came out of the speakers. Suddenly, out of the darkness, Bast's yellow, cat-shaped eyes appeared, which made Cali almost jump out of her skin.

'You are now at the threshold,' Bast whispered, adding to Cali's growing nervousness. 'The place between life and death; a liminal space between worlds, where the ghosts and demons that torment us reside. Come, we need to find the gateway.'

Cali could barely make out anything on the screen, other than the outline of the cat walking deeper into the darkness. Panic began to rise within her - it was her fear of the dark, fear of the unknown. She kept reminding herself that this was just a game, but the graphics were so real that her heartbeat grew faster in response. A full moon shone in the night sky, but there wasn't a single star to be seen. Decrepit gravestones were dotted around her, and Cali wondered at what point had the game turned into some kind of horror movie.

'Keep your vibration high and remember your affirmation. All you're seeing is a reflection of your inner mind.'

Cali recited the words. '*I am safe. I am protected and connected. I am never alone,*' over and over in her mind.

She took a step forward, looking for any clues as to where the key could be. In the distance, she noticed the outline of a woman sitting in the shadows in front of a tall iron gate. She was illuminated by a torch that hung above her head, and she was calmly stirring a large iron cauldron and muttering strange words. Cali spotted a bunch of old metal keys tied to her waistband. The woman raised her head and looked towards Cali.

'Behold, I am Hecate, Queen of the Underworld, Goddess of Witchcraft, Dark Mother and Keeper of Keys. Who approaches the crossroads?'

Cali froze. There was that word again, *witch*. She thought the whole point of the game was to move away from that horrible label - yet, instead, she was with the bloody Goddess of Witchcraft. Maybe her mum was right after all, no good would ever come from this.

'Who approaches the crossroads? You're a witch, aren't you?'

Cali couldn't even move a finger to type a response. Poppy's face flashed into her mind, taunting her. She was not a bloody witch. Cali's heart began beating as fast and loud as a techno track and her breath became shallow. She squeezed her eyes shut, hoping that the whole scene would simply go away.

'Why are you so afraid? She will sense your fear, your doubt, your denial. She will feed off it,' Bast whispered.

Cali didn't know why she was so scared, or what made the game feel so terrifyingly real. She opened her eyes and looked around her bedroom to try and calm herself. When she looked back at the screen, the woman had disappeared. Her avatar stood alone under the full moon. She looked around for Bast but couldn't see her either. Then, out of nowhere, a gigantic, black, three-headed dog leapt towards her. It growled and bared its bloodstained teeth. Thick white saliva drooled from the corner of its mouths. Just as she feared it was game over, Bast swooped by, scooping her up before the beast had a chance to take a piece of her.

The Museum
Ch 10

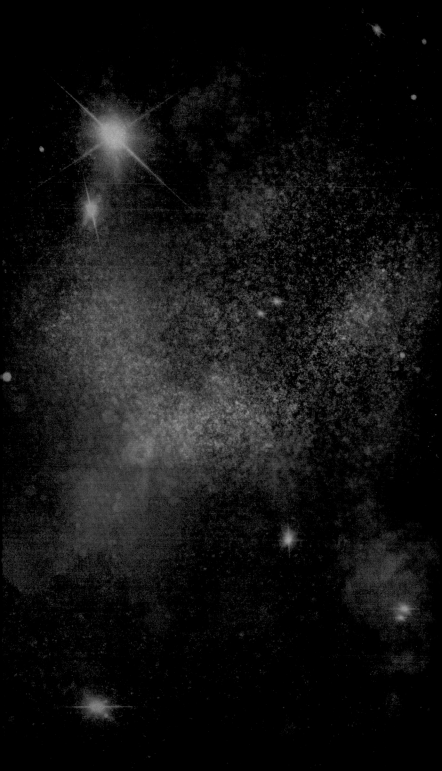

3ia and Cali stood in what was more like a rowdy mob than the orderly line commanded. Cali's eyes were wide as she took in the new surroundings. There was fidgeting, finger flicking, prodding and pushing as the volume steadily rose, echoing through the hallway.

'Evans! For the last time, BE QUIET!' exclaimed Ms Ombassu, shaking her head. 'Or you'll spend the whole trip on that coach until we head back to school.' Her words seemed to hang in the air above their heads before sinking in, producing near-silence.

Although the class had moaned about visiting yet another museum, the trip still resulted in hysteria. No longer confined to the classroom, it took seconds to smash the temporary silence as they charged through the bright white entrance hall with a force that threatened to shatter the glass ceiling.

Cali was next to Zia, who was using her phone's camera to apply a fresh layer of lipstick as the crowd rushed past. She smiled, watching as the year group suddenly shot off in all directions of the spacious lobby, leaving the parent helpers rubbing their temples and pondering escape plans. Ms Ombassu marched up behind Zia and put her hands on her daughter's shoulders to guide her through the door. Zia's cheeks flushed slightly. Cali felt a slight twinge of sadness at all the promises her mum had made to come on school trips. 'Next time.' Only each 'next time' seemed to be more impossible than the last.

Their taste of freedom was short and sweet. Ms Ombassu blew a whistle and herded the class into a long corridor that led to a private room. They filed in and found a space on the floor to sit.

'Right, now I want you to collect an information pack and follow the instructions on the task sheet carefully. You have one hour to complete all the questions and we'll meet back here. You will be working in pairs as stated, as soon as you have your partner make your way into the great hall.' Ms Ombassu didn't get to finish her sentence before the entire class began pushing their way into the marble corridor.

Cali looked down the list and was relieved to see that she'd been paired with Zia. She spotted her on the other side of the room; Zia signalled for her to hang back. They waited for the stampede to pass and bounded towards each other, Cali flashing her infectious grin.

'Hey, newbie, how about that? It's you and me, kid,' Zia said with a wink. 'I messaged you last night to see if you were okay. Are you ignoring me?'

'Ah, sorry, I only saw it this morning,' lied Cali, rather badly. 'I fell asleep early. Must have been all the excitement.'

Zia stared at her. 'Think you're going to have to do a bit better than that to fool me. You look like you haven't had a wink of sleep...your concealer won't hide those bags.'

Cali felt her cheeks flush, knowing that Zia saw straight through her.

'Come on. Spill the tea! It's me you're talking to!'

'Zia, I don't even know where to begin.' Cali looked to the heavens for help.

'You can maybe start with *what the hell happened in the classroom?*' Exactly what video evidence was Poppy so sure she had? Evidence of what?' Zia asked, staring at Cali's blank face.

'Look, I promise, I'll try to explain everything.' Cali said, nervously looking in Poppy's direction. 'But let's get started on this thing and move away from the crowd.'

'Okay. And did you know that Poppy's now spreading rumours about you being expelled from your last school?' Zia tried to gauge Cali's. 'Oh, wow, hang on a minute, you seriously did, didn't you?'

Cali pulled Zia in the opposite direction to the rest of the class. In the great hall there was an *Ancient Power and Worship* exhibition that was on tour from the British Museum. Their information pack explained that they were extremely lucky to be viewing the results of the latest archaeological dig, which had uncovered some of the most precious relics ever discovered. Cali's attention waned. Digging around in some dusty museum all day with limited supervision, while trying to avoid Poppy and her sidekick Martha, was not an appealing prospect. 'So, let's be smart here and start at the end first. That will give us a chance to avoid the crowds.' Zia touched Cali's arm gently. 'Don't worry, I'm going to be right here with you, yeah?'

Cali smiled and felt slightly more comfortable as she scanned the paper for the final question: *In ancient Egypt, as in many other ancient cultures, gods and goddesses were worshipped for their wisdom, magic, and supernatural powers. Enter the Valley of the Kings to find images and statues of the goddess. See if you can also identify the Key to the Cosmos. Draw a picture below.*

Cali felt the hairs on her arms stand to attention. *Had she read that right?* She slowly read the passage aloud.

Zia looked at her strangely. 'Hey, are you okay? You've gone kind of pale.'

'Something really weird is happening,' Cali responded, picking up her pace towards the exhibition. 'Let's get to this Valley of the Kings. I need to see something.'

Zia ran after her. When she caught up with Cali, she saw that she was resting her hands against a huge statue - a ten-foot high female figure sitting on a throne. On her head was a solar disc, and in her hand, a lotus staff carved from a smooth, dark stone.

'Eset.' Cali muttered the name under her breath.

She circled the statue, stroking its cool, smooth exterior and taking in every detail of its grandeur with delight. She noticed the symbols that adorned her dress: a triangle, a strange cross shaped key, and wings. There was a plaque at the side of the statue.

It read: *The goddess of a thousand names was known as Eset, Aset or Isis. She was a high priestess, master healer and magician. She was known as the Goddess of Transformation, which included life, birth, death and rebirth, and she's often depicted with the ancient ankh.*

'Eset?' Cali called her name then paused; it was as though time stood still. Cali's breathing slowed and she could feel her heart beating in her chest. In that exact moment, sunlight streamed down over the statue from the skylight, highlighting the ankh that was carved on Eset's dress.

Cali recalled the words Eset had spoken in the game the night before, 'These are signs that you're on the right path. We will send them to you. Trust them.' Cali sat on the floor at the statue's feet and started to giggle.

'I think we need to back up here! Do you mind telling me what on earth is happening? I'm kind of confused and worried about your mental health right now.'

'This is insane!' Cali shrieked with glee. 'Something's happening, Zia. I'm not even sure I understand it. It started when I couldn't get this pop-up advert for a game off my laptop. At first, I thought it was some kind of virus, but then a voice spoke to me and said the exact same phrase that was in the goddess book that Poppy snatched when she cornered me on the stairway...' Cali kept talking, without hesitation or need for a response. 'That's what she recorded on her phone. I nearly threw her down the stairs and they got to see my power in full force when the lasso of light brought her back.' Cali took a breath and sat down in front of the statue once again. Zia sat down on the floor beside her. 'They threatened to expose me to the whole school as some weird witch,' Cali continued. 'But this is the exact same goddess from the game. She taught me how to transform energy, so I was able to remove the video from Poppy's phone without touching it. You see, before, my negative emotions activated my powers...now they're teaching me how to control them. And now I have to face the Dark Goddess, except I don't really understand what's going on. Eset said they would always be with me and that she would send me a sign, and, well, here she is.' Cali looked back at the statue. 'This is her, the goddess from the game.'

Zia put her hands on Cali's shoulders and looked her straight in the eyes. 'I need you to breathe,' she said in a serious tone, but with a glimmer of mischief on the edges of her lips. 'First of all, that's a whole heap of info. I have, like, a million questions. First burning question, who is she?' Zia pointed to the towering statue.

'Read it for yourself, Zia, I'm not making it up. She's Eset.'

Zia pulled a funny face.

'She's basically a goddess. The mother of the universe.'

'I hate to break it to you, Cali, but goddesses aren't real. You only find them in myths or hardcore fairy stories that are a bit far-fetched and usually end up with someone eating the other and getting cursed with a head of snakes.' Zia laughed. Catching Cali's expression, she softened. 'I'm sorry, my bad. I didn't mean to make fun of you or your goddess.'

'I don't really blame you. I could hardly believe

it myself, but since I opened that game, strange things have happened. I can tell you this is not just a coincidence. Last night, this same goddess showed me a smooth, red crystal that was shaped exactly like the cross that's carved here.' Cali traced her hands over the symbol. 'I was supposed to get it in the game, but I couldn't manage to. She told me to watch for the signs.'

'Hang on, this is sounding crazier by the second. Do you actually have to find one in real life? It looks like it's called an ankh...' Zia said, reading the sign.

'Yes, it is,' came a voice from behind them. Zia smiled without turning round; she knew it was her mum. 'Otherwise known as the knot of Eset. It's a symbol of the key to heaven and earth, said to contain a secret code that transmits sacred knowledge that can give normal humans superhuman powers, and ultimately lead them to the divine. It's wonderful to see you have such an interest in it, Cali.' Ms Ombassu smiled at her.

Cali looked embarrassed, but she was unable to tear her attention away from the statue.

'It seems you have a thing for goddesses, Cali. Does your mum like them too? She named you in honour of the goddess, right?' Ms Ombassu's question was met with a blank stare. She continued, 'Kali with a 'K' is a powerful, dark goddess, the destroyer of illusion, protector of children.'

Cali was unable to speak. *How on earth did Ms Ombassu know so much about the goddesses?*

'Sorry, I can see from your face I'm clearly not making any sense to you!'

Cali eventually found her tongue. 'Actually, I've learned a bit about goddesses recently, but the idea that my mum has anything to do with them is just crazy. She's not into things like that at all, she's always too busy working and spends her time being stressed.'

'Well, it looks like the path has found you anyway,' said Ms Ombassu. 'The goddesses work in mysterious ways, as you will find out later in class this week. If you're drawn to them, maybe you've been chosen.'

Zia watched their awkward interaction and noticed the colour drain from Cali's face. She grabbed her friend's arm. 'Mum, I think we need to go back over some of the other questions on the worksheet. There might be something we missed.'

Ms Ombassu pointed at a question on her daughter's paper. 'Well, I see you found the ankh. It's the bridge between heaven and earth.'

Cali looked blankly at Ms Ombassu, then once more at the statue. 'The bridge?'

'Yes, it's the key that connects us to the goddesses. Right, girls, you've got twenty-five minutes left. It's nice to chat to you properly, Cali with a 'C'.'

As Cali backed away from the statue, reluctantly, she whispered under her breath, 'Okay, Eset, you've got my attention. I can see and feel you in my world, just as much as I can when I enter The Queendom. Now, show me what I need to see, guide me to the key.'

As Cali and Zia left the room, they failed to notice two figures hidden behind a tall cabinet in the corner near the door. Once they were safely out of view, Poppy and Martha laughed out loud.

'Well, well, well, this is epic. I can't wait to see the shock on her weird little witchy face when she knows we heard everything.'

*

When the class gathered at the end of the day, Ms Ombassu addressed them all in the private room. 'Are we ready for the big reveal?'

She was barely able to contain her excitement.

The silence from the class didn't deter her in the slightest, as her fingers clutched the dark material cover that was draped over large plastic trays. 'You have no idea how incredibly lucky we are to be seeing these artefacts first-hand. This is such an honour.'

The class swarmed around the tables. Cali and Zia had thoroughly reviewed all their findings, searching for more clues about the goddesses. They'd been among the last to come back and now found themselves at the back with limited view. Through the crowd, Cali saw that Poppy had a front row spot. She turned and their eyes met; Poppy gave her such a sickly, sinister smile it made her shudder.

'I present to you this exclusive viewing opportunity from the latest archaeological dig, which culminated only a few months ago in Luxor, from the Valley of the Kings. This is a selection of incredibly rare relics, never before seen in public.' Ms Ombassu dramatically removed the cloth. The class's response failed to match her awe.

'I have no idea why my mum gets so embarrassingly excited about a heap of broken junk,' Zia whispered under her breath, her hand covering her mouth to hide her amusement.

'You're lucky, my mum doesn't get excited about anything - ever. She doesn't even know I exist.'

Ms Ombassu and the museum guide proceeded to handle all the different artefacts. They wore white gloves as they picked each of the relics up, discussing every detail of their merits and meanings. The increasing noise and fidgeting from the students indicated their distraction and distinct lack of interest.

Suddenly, a voice cut through the hum of casual conversation and chatter. 'This might interest you, Cali, it's the ankh.'

Cali heard her loud and clear. She scanned the collection of golden objects and recognised the outline of the ankh and the smooth red crystal embedded in its centre. It was exactly the same as the one she'd seen in the game.

She tugged on Zia's sleeve. 'It's the one, it's the key.' Cali made her way to the front of the table to get a closer look. She couldn't take her eyes off the precious object as she studied its smooth exterior. This was, without a doubt, the sign Eset had spoken of, the key she needed if she was ever going to get back into The Queendom and complete her mission. But the chances of her having it were pretty much zero in a billion. She glanced up to see Poppy watching her like a hawk.

There was something in her eyes that made Cali feel like she was being hunted. Even though she'd spent most of the day trying to be invisible, it seemed to make Poppy want to find her even more. What was it about her that always attracted this kind of unwanted attention? What could a girl like Poppy - who had absolutely everything: money, confidence, good looks, and an amazing lifestyle with pools and private jets that she flaunted on social media - possibly want from her?

Descent into Darkness
Ch 11

To complete their museum visit, the class was allowed to spend the last fifteen minutes of the trip in the gift shop. The whole year group rifled through the shop's treasures and trinkets for something to waste money on. Most were gathered around the stationery stand, where there were fancy fountain pens and graphite pencils with the museum's name and logo, and erasers shaped like artefacts.

Cali was drawn to a glass cabinet at the back of the shop near the cash register. The piece in centre stage, encased beneath a spotlight, was none other than a replica of the ankh. It seemed as though time once again stood still around her. She felt a tingle down her spine as she watched the way the light reflected the different facets of the crystal.

Then she heard Eset's voice. 'You are never alone. I will help you face your fears. You were born for this.' An involuntary tear rolled down Cali's cheek. No matter how scared she felt, which seemed to be pretty much most of the time right now, she was incredibly lucky that at least someone was there for her.

'Excuse me, can I just get in front of you there?' The question startled Cali from her daydream. The shop assistant unlocked the cabinet and scooped out the ankh. 'It's a beauty, isn't it?'

'Yes, it is,' Cali responded. She followed her as she laid it out by the till on a black velvet pouch.

'Oh, wow, can you actually believe it? We agree on something at long last!' said Poppy sarcastically. She ushered Cali to move out of the way with a dismissive wave of her hand.

'Just so you know,' the museum assistant said to Poppy, 'this arrived in the shop today.' She seemed young but she had a grey streak down the centre of her otherwise dark brown hair. 'And it's not a toy! This is a limited-edition replica of the crystal ankh that was found most recently in Luxor. It has 14kt gold plating and a semi-precious red crystal.' She peered over the top of her glasses in a way that made Cali back away from the counter.

'Wonderful. And how much is it?' asked Poppy, with such confidence and clarity that the assistant instantly changed her demeanor and responded to her like she was an adult.

'It's £249.99.'

'Maybe a little bit more than your pocket money, Cali, don't you think?' remarked Poppy loudly. She and Martha giggled.

Cali felt her cheeks flush. 'Oh no, it's fine. I mean, I'm not interested in buying it, I'm just happy to admire it.'

'Don't be silly, Cali, I can see how much it means to you. It's the key to The Queendom, isn't it?'

Cali froze as her mind went into overdrive. *How on earth did she know? What was going on? She must have overheard somehow, she must have been listening...* Her face gave away every one of her fears.

'Oh my god. Or should I say, goddess? I wonder what you would do to get your little witchy hands on this key.'

Cali looked at her speechless, and muttered, 'I'm just happy to look at it.'

She tried to move past them, but Poppy grabbed her arm tightly, digging every one of her manicured nails into her skin. 'Come on, we both know that's not true. The truth is, you can't afford it. Maybe we should call you 'Charity Case Cali' from now on!' Laughter came from all around them.

The girls were head-to-head, energy firing like lasers between them. It had happened so quickly that Cali had been caught off guard. She didn't have time to think about any kind of protection. Poppy's words stung and the embarrassment burned Cali's cheeks; they could only be cooled by a fresh flow of tears. As Cali tried to yank her arm free, she felt Poppy's nails dig in even deeper.

'Girls! What's going on over there?' Ms Ombassu shouted, her head appearing over the crowd from the other side of the shop.

'Nothing, Miss,' responded Poppy, releasing her grip on Cali. Now free, Cali pushed past the crowd towards the front of the shop. But Poppy did not give up. She swiftly followed after her; once outside in the hallway, she inched closer.

'You've been so obsessed with that bloody old bit of stone, you haven't even noticed your friend is missing. That's not very good of you now, is it, Cali? Not very caring. Especially after what she's done for you.' Poppy was in her element, dramatising every sentence with expressive lifts of her badly-painted-on eyebrows. 'You'd have been so proud. She acted ever so bravely when we told her we'd got you cornered in the toilets! Think she wanted to try and save you. Not sure exactly how you've managed to fool her into some kind of deluded loyalty.'

'What have you done to Zia?' demanded Cali. 'I don't know what you think you're playing at, but you need to tell me, right now.'

'What would be the fun in that?' Poppy responded, her arms crossed over her chest.

Cali thought she heard Zia's voice. She saw her bag outside a door further down the corridor. Poppy just laughed. Cali pushed past her and ran to the room. It was pitch black and Cali groped the walls for the light switch but couldn't find one. She sensed that she was in a small area. As her eyes adjusted to the dark, she realised that she was in some kind of storage room filled with shelves and lots of boxes stacked up.

'Zia, where are you?' she called out, but there was no response. Cali was confused. Zia's bag was right outside, but Zia definitely wasn't here. She realised that she'd fallen for some kind of prank. She turned to open the door and found it was locked from the outside. She tried it again but it didn't budge. She kicked herself for being so gullible.

She banged on the door, shouting, 'Hello, can anyone hear me? I'm locked in!'

She glanced round the strange, claustrophobic space and wished she was anywhere else but here, in the dark. 'Not the darkness, anything but the darkness,' Cali pleaded internally, her fingers frantically feeling the walls for a light switch but finding nothing. The bus would leave without her, though her mother probably wouldn't even notice she was gone. Who knew how long she'd be trapped there?

She gasped and tried to inhale as much as possible, as though the air may soon run out. It made her feel lightheaded and she slipped down the wall into a heap on the floor, clutching her knees. 'Is there anyone out there who can help me?' she pleaded.

She suddenly heard Eset's voice inside her mind. 'You are never alone, we're always here with you. You just need to connect and command.'

Cali instinctively concentrated on her breath and instructed it to slow down. She tried to force her mind to do the same and focused on her heart. Eset had said that her thoughts wouldn't magically disappear; she had to let them float by in her mind like clouds in the sky. Her thoughts felt like heavy rain clouds; she worried that she would be trapped there forever. She was so full of self-pity that the rain clouds burst and tears streamed down her face.

You're doing it wrong, Cali screamed at herself. *It's supposed to be easy!*

Then she remembered to keep her attention on her breathing. She took a deep, slow breath, then another, then another. Before she knew it, her heart felt like it was expanding. Her body began to feel lighter, her breathing no longer forced. She felt as if she was leaving the darkness of the cupboard behind.

She could see herself in her mind's eye, surrounded by a bright light that glowed like a thousand candles.

Even though she couldn't make out their faces, she knew the goddesses surrounded her, creating a circle of light. She could feel how they were infusing the light with their emotions, and deep waves of unconditional love washed over her.

Eset stepped forward and embraced her. 'Your connection is growing stronger, and you are seeing the signs, yes?'

Cali nodded.

'I understand that your fear feels very real, but please know that every time you return to The Queendom, we will move forward together on your mission.' Eset handed her one end of a red thread; the other end went over the edge and into the abyss.

'Take this first step. Meet her. The Dark Goddesses are our sisters, but their domain is in the shadows of the underworld. They're summoned whenever you need to integrate aspects of yourself that you are denying, hiding, or resisting. Whatever it is about her that frightens or repulses you exists within you too. She is only a mirror.'

Cali willed her trembling feet to take a small step forward, then another. She gripped the red thread with her eyes squeezed tightly shut.

'Open your eyes.'

She heard the words in surround sound, but refused to obey. The deep darkness below was waiting to swallow her whole. She wasn't brave enough to let go or to open her eyes. She didn't want to go down there, she didn't know what she would find. She didn't think she'd survive. Her sensitivity was razor-sharp, and it threatened to rip her to shreds. She felt her heart booming, blood rushing, fists clenching, palms sweating, mouth gasping for air. Balancing on the edge, she knew she wouldn't be able to hold on for much longer.

'Don't make me go down there. I'm not ready. It all feels like too much for me,' Cali pleaded. Her toes lost their grip and her eyes sprung open. She was falling through space, spiralling down, deeper down, into complete darkness. Then she reached a surface.

She was back in the underworld. This time, she could hear the cry of a child. The child seemed lost and terrified. Her emotions were too strong to handle and she felt a heavy sadness begin to well in the pit of her stomach. Cali could see nothing as her eyes struggled to adjust to the darkness; she could only hear the piercing cry echoing around her.

Cali felt that she had to be in some sort of cave and got to her feet. She stroked the stone walls; she could make out smooth areas and sharp edges. She took a step forward, and as she did so, she sensed the Dark Goddess was near. The thought that flashed through her mind was that, maybe, this wicked witch devoured children. If Cali didn't defeat her, she could be next.

The Dark Goddess was suddenly before her - a large, hooded figure with three heads. One looked to the left, the other to the right, and the last one looked directly at her. All had the same hollow jet-black eyes. The head nearest to Cali was covered in tribal tattoos and had black pointed horns, like those of a devil, protruding from the sides of its slender, pale white face. The goddess's many arms were moving in all directions. In one of her six hands she held a snake; in another, a torch. She held a dagger in another hand and in another, the keys. Cali felt every bone in her body tremble uncontrollably. She urged herself to wake from the nightmare. Even returning to the confines of the dark, locked cupboard at the museum would have been a relief.

'I am Hecate, your tormentor, but also your protector. Both The Gatekeeper and your guide. I am The Nightwalker, but also the light of all things. Nothing is ever as it first seems.'

Hecate threw objects into a large, iron cauldron on a roaring, open fire: plants, flowers and herbs, liquids poured from green glass bottles, then a feather and a rabbit's foot. As each item dropped into the pot, a red and violet flame arose, crackling against the moonlit sky.

'Witchcraft is not to be feared. It is, and always has been, medicine. Natural healing. I'm the hidden power within that's now awakening in you, and in many other girls and women across the world. To deny the inner witch is to deny the deeper world. The more you resist me, the more persistent and terrifying I become.'

Cali controlled her breath and recited the mantra, 'I am safe. I am protected and connected. I am never alone.' She said it over and over, like it was on a loop in her mind, despite it being the least safe or protected she'd ever felt in her life. She squeezed her eyes shut. 'Bring me from darkness to light, into the light. Help me back. Please help me.'

Cali felt someone touch her arm, which made her scream.

'Cali, it's okay! It's Zia, it's okay.'

Cali opened her eyes and squinted against the light streaming in from the open door. Zia reached to pull her up.

'Where have you been?' Cali asked. 'I thought I was trapped here. Poppy tricked me into running after you.'

'I know,' said Zia. 'She sent me on a wild-goose chase, too. We can hash all that out later. Right now, we've got to run or the coach will leave without us.'

*

Outside, the whole class was pushing and shoving to get on the coach, so they could choose the best seats."Come on, class, we're late!' called Ms Ombassu. 'Let's not waste any more time.'

Cali stood in a daze on the pavement, watching the other kids, wondering why everything was so competitive. Zia grabbed her by the arm and elbowed their way through the crowd to the steps. Once on board, she strategically selected seats a few rows from the front. Close enough to the teachers to get help, yet far enough away to share secrets.

'Are you sure you don't want me to tell?' Zia asked. 'That crazy psycho sent me round half the museum looking for you while she had you locked in a bloody cupboard. You could have been there all night if I hadn't found you.'

Cali didn't respond, she just stared out the window. Words escaped her. Her mind was racing. Then Poppy appeared on the coach and proceeded to waltz down the aisle with Martha and the rest of her entourage. Before she could utter a word, Zia stood, ready to meet her.

'I'm warning you, don't! Do not even go there.' Zia waved a finger dismissively in Poppy's face.

'Ooh, touchy. Has someone upset you, darling?' Poppy smiled her usual sickly, sarcastic smile, before raising her chin even higher and sauntering past.

Cali couldn't help but think what a waste. What was the point of Poppy's perfect smile when it was never genuine? She exhaled, not even aware she'd been holding her breath.

'It's okay when you're here,' Cali said quietly to Zia. 'You're not scared to stand up to her. I seriously don't know what her problem is. She has it in for me, big time.'

'You know what I think it is? It's because you're different. You're...I don't know, special, somehow. They sense that about you and it frightens them.'

Cali blushed and the corners of her mouth crept into a shy smile. Her eyes remained transfixed on the lines of her palm; she examined their grooves and wondered whether, if she rubbed them hard enough, she could change her destiny.

'It's always been this way. I guess I've always been different. It makes people uncomfortable.'

'No, Cali, that's not true. Only in certain circles. You know, all these girls want to look the same, wear the same labels, like a specific type of music, to be obsessed with similar kinds of boys, gossip about the same gossip...it's like you're only socially acceptable if you're a clone. If you hate on yourself and other girls. It's become like a badge of honour.' She took hold of Cali's hands before she continued. 'We're not like them and never will be, and I'm happy we're not. They're stuck up and bland...and, underneath it all, most likely unhappy and insecure.'

Cali exhaled and released all the tension in her system. She could see herself in Zia's eyes. The rest of the journey flew by as they chatted. Cali had never met anyone quite like Zia, she was like a breath of fresh air. Zia had such a childlike, playful energy that it made Cali realise she'd become way too serious. For a few moments, her usual heaviness, worry and panic was replaced with a sense of peace.

Home Ground
Ch 12

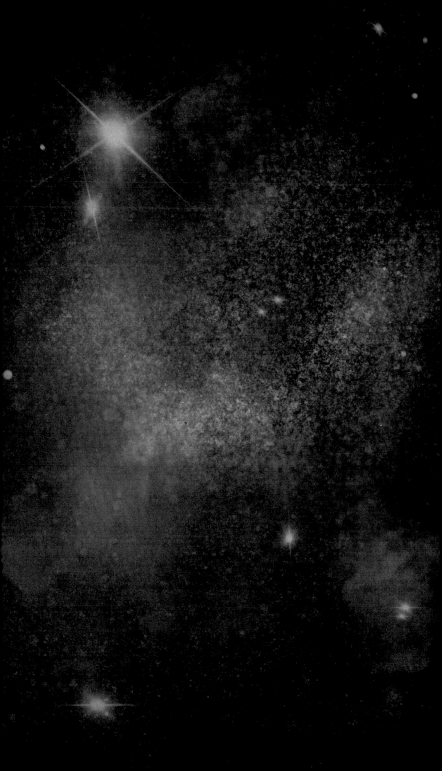

As Cali walked down the familiar street that led to her house, she noticed how the darkness was creeping in earlier than usual. The autumn nights must be happy, now they're dominating the day again, she thought. She stopped outside their front window and peered in. Nobody had moved from their seats at either side of the room to turn on the ceiling light, so the scene was lit only by electronic devices. She was relieved and excited to see the hypnotic glow from behind the laptop screen illuminating her dad as he sat in his battered leather recliner. He was finally back from working overseas. Her mum was in her usual spot, perched on the edge of her bright retro dining stool that she swore would bring us a lot of money one day. Cali found it hilarious that they complained about how long she spent online when they were both more addicted to their devices than she was.

As Cali quietly opened the door to the living room she could hear the tap, tap, tapping of fingers on laptops. There was also noise from a discarded iPad, of some YouTube presenter unboxing toys. Eva had instead turned her attention to a selection of black and white Barbie dolls that she was playing with under the table.

'Is there a reason you're all sat in the dark?' Cali switched on the light and threw her blazer and bag on the floor. She sensed there had already been a fight from the tense, frosty atmosphere. At the sound of her voice, Rocco came bounding over. He proceeded to jump up and down, demanding to be greeted with a tummy rub.

Cali felt relieved to see her dad in his usual spot, even if her mum wasn't as pleased about his return. She had to restrain herself from running over and jumping onto his knee, like she might have done when she was younger.

'Hey, baby, come over here and let me see you. How was school today?' her dad asked. His prominent brown eyes peered above his laptop screen and he flashed her a warm, encouraging smile. Her dad had been away for what seemed like forever. His job was in tech for a global development project and he'd been working in South Africa. People always told her that she looked just like him, which was endlessly embarrassing. She recognised his smile as her own, and was happy she had the same full lips. His rich, brown, freckled skin had a warm tone, which gave his round face a lovely glow. Cali noted a few silver specks had appeared in his short, shaved hair since the last time she'd seen him.

He wore an old navy pinstripe suit and black polished shoes. He wasn't vain and didn't like to be flashy, but one thing about him was that he loved a good pair of shoes. They had to fit well and they had to be shiny, and he made sure everyone knew they came from a specialist shoemaker on Bond Street. Even in this serious outfit, he couldn't mask his mischievousness, his boyish essence.

'Fine, Dad.' Cali responded in the best way she knew to make him happy. 'I got an A in my science test.'

'An A?!' He stopped typing and reached out to playfully punch her arm. 'Well done, baby, that's great. I'm so proud of you. Just look how big and beautiful you're getting.'

He smiled so widely that his cheeks made two little brown apples, only the smile never reached his eyes. When he glanced over at Cali's mum, it vanished instantly.

Cali had noticed that, lately, his cheerfulness seemed to be reserved for her and her little sister. The minute he and her mum spoke, it would evaporate. Cali couldn't remember things being this bad in London, where their occasional fights would usually end with them howling with laughter. There wasn't any laughter right now.

'How long are you back for, Dad?' Cali hoped his smile might reappear.

'Um, just ten days this time,' he said in a hushed tone. 'They urgently need me back.'

'Ten days?!' came Mum's shrill voice from the other side of the room. 'Bloody hell, Trevor, when were you going to mention that little detail to me? Only ten days at home this time?'

Cali looked at her mum. Her face was getting redder by the second. She turned back to her dad, who had disappeared from view behind his laptop screen.

'I thought it was supposed to be four weeks,' her mum continued. 'You told me you were definitely going to be around to help this time. It's like you think everything in the house and with the kids gets done by magic.' Cali could see her mum was trembling with anger, which was sending shockwaves through her skin.

'It just can't be helped this time, Corinne. It's a crucial point in the project and I'm needed. I have to go back to work early.'

'What about your family? I work too, you know, and bloody hard, not that that seems to count for anything around here. I don't know how you expect me to cope on my own.' She shot up from her chair and the laptop she'd forgotten was on her lap crashed to the floor. Cali held her breath as the drama reached a crescendo.

Unspoken pain and the build-up of past anger, abandonment and confusion fizzed in the air. Cali felt all the emotions surge through her veins, their intensity jolting her. She would have given anything to stop the hurt.

Her father sat in silence as her mum left the room, letting the door slam shut behind her.

Cali dropped to her knees and crawled under the table to check on Eva, who sat with her hands over her ears, surrounded by her multicultural, plastic soap opera. There was a black Ken doll, a merman and three mixed race babies sitting in her mum's heels, while a blonde Barbie and one with curves and an afro were driving a bright pink convertible car.

'They've been fighting again,' said Eva.

'About the usual?'

'Money and your school, Cali. Mama was crying again.'

'I thought so,' whispered Cali. 'Try not to worry, baby, you know they always work it out, no matter how bad it seems.' She gave her sister a kiss on the top of her head, her lips briefly nestling in Eva's bouncy curls. Cali closed her eyes and inhaled the smell of her fruity hair cream.

'Will you play Barbies with me?' her sister asked with a cute tilt of her head, always wanting to make the most of any attention that came her way.

'Not right now, Eva.'

'Later then? Do you promise?'

'Yes, I promise.'

Cali gazed at her dad and realised he'd gone straight back to whatever work he was distracting himself with. She felt she should go after her mum and quietly left the room.

As she entered the kitchen, her mum was at the sink, clanging pans and dishes. 'Hey," she finally managed, without looking up. 'Did you have a good day at school?'

'Yes, Mum,' Cali lied, her head going over the events of the day that she so desperately wanted to understand and share. She swallowed them all down. It wasn't a good time to burden her mum. 'It was fun. We had the trip to the museum.'

'Shoot! That was today? Was I supposed to give you some extra money?' she asked.

Cali saw that her eyes were red-rimmed from crying. She almost looked right through Cali, with a sort of vacant stare. 'No, it was fine. I took some savings I had in my room,' Cali lied again. Her mum turned away and ran her hands through her hair. Her body crumpled over the kitchen counter as she began to cry. Cali felt helpless as the sound of her mum's sobs washed through the house.

Cali felt an urge to put her arms around her and tell her everything was going to be alright, but as she looked at her mum, she worried that it would be difficult to convince her. As if she read Cali's mind, her mum pulled her gently towards her heaving chest. She wrapped her arms tightly around her daughter and spoke softly into her hair.

'I'm sorry. I'm sorry for not being there for you, for all the arguing, for all the chaos. It's just, people like us, we're not made for this world.' Her mum paused, as if she was going to say something else then thought better of it. 'Things are a bit challenging for Mummy right now, but I'll work harder. I'll try harder. It's going to be okay.'

Cali didn't know what to believe. Her senses told her the true story.

The Shadow
Ch 13

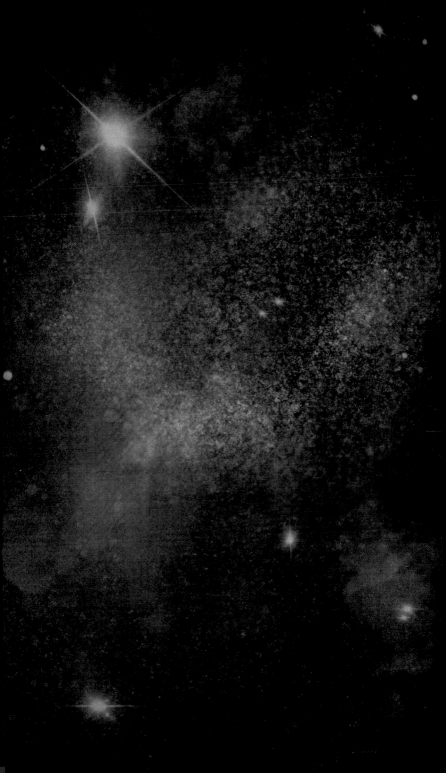

Cali climbed up into the comfy confines of the top bunk. Despite being snuggled in her cocoon, she couldn't soothe her overactive mind. A hundred questions ran riot inside, each one talking over the other, vying for attention, hanging around and clouding her mind like hungry ghosts.

The vacant look in her mum's eyes, and the way she'd broken down in front of her, were etched in Cali's memory. It left Cali shattered that she couldn't fix things. *Was Mum going to be okay? What would happen between her and Dad? How was Cali supposed to help Eva when she couldn't even help herself? How could she make the bullying stop? What about her mission and the key? How was she ever going to get it?*

Cali knew only one way to silence them. She plugged in her earpods, flipped open her laptop and clicked on the words 'The Queendom' on her desktop. She felt her whole body soften as the game opened up and the beautiful, bright, starry skyscape filled the screen. She watched as the ankh spun on screen and couldn't help but think it was taunting her. It had been right under her nose, yet completely out of reach. Now it turned up practically everywhere she looked. She felt agitation in her chest, which made her fidget. Cali didn't understand. She'd seen the signs, received the guidance and had come so close to the key twice today - and still it evaded her.

She remembered Ms Ombassu's words, that the ankh was the bridge between heaven and earth, and that it would give the holder special powers. The key was going to unlock something in Cali that she needed, then she'd know exactly what to say to make her mum feel better. She would be able to handle her emotions and stand up to Poppy. The key could be the answer to all her prayers. When she was a Light Warrior, maybe she'd have the power to be brave and popular and she'd finally fit in.

Cali saw the sleek outline of Bast against the full moon and zoomed in to see her feline face.

'Hey, girl, good to see you're back.' Bast spoke in a soft, purring tone. 'You get five stars just for returning. We have a very important session today. It's time for you to truly understand what's at stake, here in The Queendom, and the real darkness we're up against. You're going to get a special peek into the place no one can ever enter—The Nerve Centre.' There was some interference on screen, signaling an incoming live transmission. When it cleared, Eset appeared on screen.

'If you're to join forces with the goddesses as a true warrior of the light, you must know the evil we all face.' Eset stood in what looked like a high-tech control centre, with monitors and buttons filling the wall space. In the centre there was a stone altar and a huge crystal globe. Cali gazed into it, but all she could see was a cloudy mist.

'In the Nerve Centre we watch and see everything in your world and carefully monitor the impact of all your actions on the heartbeat of the Earth.' The camera panned round and Cali saw that the room was filled with many different goddesses, together with other, different kinds of beings; all were gathered around the crystal globe. There were beings made entirely of light, winged beings, alien-like beings, beings that were part animal, and giant angels huddled together.

'What you're seeing is a gathering of the archangels, ascended masters, and trusted guardians of the galaxy, who constantly watch over, and pray for, your planet.'

Cali noticed a heart rate monitor, which gave a constant reading of the Earth's pulse. She realised that the TV screens surrounding those gathered together were showing real-time footage of global

Bast

events. The screens were filled with images of people fighting, stealing, looting and polluting, their faces as furious as the fires that surrounded them. They showed people as predators, hunting and killing animals, and even each other; people poisoning the seas with plastic, oil and chemicals. They were digging up fields and forestland, building concrete jungles and skyscrapers, depleting and destroying Earth. People flew on private jets and hoarded money as children starved. The worst possible news stories, like those her dad watched and her mum complained about, combined in one, vicious onslaught.

As Cali took in the scenes, she felt overwhelmed- her senses overloaded with a heaviness that only a spontaneous flood of tears could hope to wash away. She felt such deep pain, she thought she might actually be sick.

'Empaths are strong feelers of feelings,' said Eset 'It means you feel things on a deeper level than most other people. Injustice, meanness, cruelty, harm- especially to animals and the environment-these destructive acts cut you deeply. Your tears are the tears of the Earth. Each time more of the forest is slaughtered, or the water is poisoned, you feel that the pain is yours. For that reason, you must always protect and ground your energy.'

'What has all of this got to do with the game?' Cali typed, genuinely confused.

'Learning the ways of the Light Warrior is no game. Think of it as a training ground.' Eset's tone was serious. 'You came to the higher realm to learn how to raise your own vibration. You go down to the underworld to face your shadow. Then you go out into Middle Earth to practise raising the frequency of the planet.'

Cali looked at Bast, who was beside Eset, watching everything.

'In The Queendom, you can clearly see and sense a

person's true vibration. There are those who spread higher vibrations of love and who help balance the lower, denser energies like doubt, anger and fear. There are many difficult situations on Earth.'

As Cali looked closer at the images in front of her. It was clear that every person had their own personal glow surrounding them. On even closer inspection, Cali saw that these were made up of different colours, like a rainbow prism. There were also tears, rips and dark spots within the prism.

'There's a lot of polarity on your planet. There has been, and always will be, the light and the dark. The darkness is not something to be afraid of; it exists in all of us to be integrated. But when it is denied, disowned, judged and feared, it creates problems. If the shadow is not brought to the light, a person's inner demons grow. They get louder and attack their mind, suppress their emotions and harden their heart. We call this calcification. You can see it in their energy field, in the light around their body, which is called their aura. Once their aura is affected, they can spread their low vibration to others. These low-level energies combine and spiral into crimes, violence and wars.'

A scene flashed up that showed violence erupting in an American street. Cali could see how everyone involved was shrouded by an accumulating shadow that got darker and denser. 'How can we heal the pain?' she asked.

'Those who want to be healed, can be, but for those entrenched in darkness, it's more difficult. It can be far more dangerous,' said Eset, sadly.

'How does the shadow get into people? Are we born with it? Or do we catch it from somewhere?'

'The shadow in people is often passed down to them from their parents. or it's imprinted from something that happened to them when they were young. Instead of feeling that emotion and releasing it from the energetic body, it's pushed down, hidden and ignored.'

'What happens when a person just seems lost? Like, they aren't themselves anymore...they're not the person you once knew?' Cali asked.

'We give people many opportunities to heal the shadow, but sometimes they choose to ignore the invitations. They're afraid that the pain of dealing with it will be far greater than the pain of hiding it. But that's not the case. It takes up far more energy and lifeforce to hide than it does to heal. Is there someone you're specifically thinking of?'

'My mum,' replied Cali softly.

'Let's take a look, shall we? Enter her name and date of birth and I'll see how she's doing.'

Cali entered her mother's details, but immediately felt worried and that she shouldn't have said anything.

Before she could change her mind, Eset swept her hands across the crystal globe and stared intently into the mist. 'Ah, this is a woman with a very pure heart. She's had an intimate relationship with the Dark Goddess in the past. Unfortunately, she's strayed far from her true path. This denial and avoidance may have cost her dearly. We've provided many opportunities for her to awaken to the light, but her fear has grown in intensity through your ancestral line. She does not look strong enough to heal this by herself. She's going to need your help, Cali.'

Suddenly, Cali had a flashback to the look in her mum's eyes when she'd said, 'People like us weren't meant for this world.' Maybe there was more to her mum's fear of the dark than she let on. Could it be that she'd also been asked to face the Dark Goddess?

'What can I do to help her?' Cali asked, feeling overwhelmed again.

'There's no need to worry. You're doing everything

you can. By walking this path and healing your own shadow, you have the power to heal seven generations into the future and seven generations into the past.' Eset clapped her hands to clear the globe then swept them over its surface once again. 'Now, let me show you what happens when we spread the light of love. This light is a thousand times more powerful.' Eset smiled as a video clip showed people coming together at a peaceful protest; they held candles and walked together in solidarity with hand drawn placards, demanding change and praying for peace. The light around them was bright and intensely beautiful.

'This is what you and the other Light Warriors are here to do on Earth.' Eset smiled encouragingly into the camera. 'In its simplest form, the purpose of The Queendom is to teach you how to spread the light while loving, healing and integrating the shadow. We cannot fight the darkness. That only makes it grow and spread further. We must embrace the shadow, so it can be healed and brought into the light.' Eset clapped her hands again and the images in the crystal globe faded away until it showed a clear surface.

'Remember, your sensitivity is not your weakness, it's your power. The world needs you exactly as you are. The future of The Queendom and that of the world depends on you claiming this power. Now, you must go with Bast to the crystalline core. She will help you prepare to meet the Dark Goddess and claim your first key.

The Crystals
Ch 14

With one click they arrived in a gigantic cavern encrusted with sparkling crystals that were as ancient as the Earth itself. Bast flew around the roof of the cave then landed, opening her wings and puffing out her silky, black chest proudly.

'Welcome to the crystalline core at the very centre of the earth, home to the sacred ruby heart stone. During your missions in the underworld, it's a safe, protected space to ground your energy and come back to your centre.'

Cali switched to a 360-degree view, so that she could explore every part of the cave. The walls glistened as they reflected the small shaft of silver moonlight above them. To the right were rails of costumes; it was a girl's dressing up dream. Jewel-plated body armour and hooded capes, in vibrant rainbow shades, hung above neat rows of winged boots. Before Cali could even ask the question, Bast gave the answer. 'Astral boots. You'll find out more about them later. They allow you to fly, and even transcend time. But, girl, come over here and check out these costumes.'

Cali browsed the outfits and selected a red, sparkly suit with a matching cloak. She dragged it across to her avatar to make the change. The avatar gazed back at Cali, and it was everything she wanted to be: tall, strong and beautiful, with long flowing hair.

'Yeah, you know you look great. Now, raise your hands above your head and stretch your arms and legs out wide, to make the letter X.' Cali did as instructed, but secretly wished that the screen was a mirror so she could admire her new self a little longer. 'Perfect, that's right. This is what we call a power pose. It's a posture that amplifies your confidence.'

'Come over here, there's something really important I need to show you. When the sacred cave calls to you, it connects you to the crystal stone spirits. We receive our healing here.' Bast walked towards two golden

135

treasure chests at the far side of the cave. 'One of the most important things in this realm is our relationship with the natural world...the elementals, the fae folk, the tree spirits. You can communicate with them - they have so much wisdom to share.' Bast jumped gracefully onto one of the chests. 'The stone people are my favourites to work with. They're the oldest and wisest beings, as ancient as the planets. They'll give everything they have to help you. In this first chest are the shadow stones; they take and transmute all of the darkest emotions, thoughts, fears and beliefs anyone could ever have. Pain, anger, guilt, shame...they're emotions that have a very dense energy and the lowest vibration. When you put your hand inside the chest you're able to release them and let them go. They wash away.'

Cali felt a little apprehensive. She didn't know what would happen next. The lid flung open and she admired the dark crystals and stones of all shapes and sizes. As she edged closer, she could hear groaning and crying coming from the crystals, as if the chest was some kind of torture chamber.

'Come closer and hold both your hands out in front of you,' said Bast. 'Ask the question, *what do I need to let go of that's blocking me or holding me back?* There's no need to do anything, the crystals will choose you, based on what's inside of you.'

Cali instructed her avatar to open its hands. Two crystals jumped out and landed in her palms. She watched them closely. The small, smooth, black one was wailing, and the dark purple, jagged one was jumping up and down and snarling.

'Interesting. How perfect,' said Bast, curiously. 'Fear of being your true self, which manifests as feeling very unsafe on the earth. This can attract people and situations to you that make you feel vulnerable and exposed. Also, we have some anger here, mainly aimed at your mother.' Bast winked. 'Don't worry, the crystals will begin to absorb your negative energy.'

'Put the crystals into the pouch on your belt. You must not touch them again until you meet the Dark Goddess. They will be your offering to her.' Cali did as instructed.

'What's in the other chest?' Cali asked.

'That chest contains the most potent and powerful crystals in the realm. All crystals have an enormous amount of love for people of the earth. They're here to give you all the extra support and assistance you could possibly need.' Bast opened the second chest and Cali gasped. It was full of beautiful, glowing crystals of all shapes and sizes. 'Again, hold your hands out and allow the crystals to choose you. The right crystal will always find its way to you.'

Cali did as she was told, and watched as three crystals jumped right out of the chest and landed in her avatar's hands. One was a deep red colour, one was shiny and black, and the other was a shimmering, iridescent white crystal.

'Perfect!' said Bast, as she identified them. 'Red jasper is a powerful, grounding crystal that works with earth energies, spirits and guardians. A stone of empowerment that promotes a sense of power and self-confidence when faced with bullies. These crystals are the best protective talismans for warriors.' Bast appeared excited. 'And black tourmaline is my personal favourite. It works like a psychic shield to deflect destructive forces and neutralise negative thoughts and worries.' It sounded like the answer to all of Cali's problems.

Bast turned her attention to the last crystal. 'We also have this beautiful, white selenite to help you connect and hear celestial guidance. To clear and seal your aura.'

Cali held the three crystals in her avatar's hand, and with one click, put them all in its chest pocket, close to its heart.

'Keep the crystals close to your body at all times,' said Bast. She looked lovingly into the chest before closing it. 'They will constantly be working for you.' Cali looked around the cave and saw a row of seats carved into the surface of the rock. There were also some space-age-type masks connected to long, silver tubes above them.

'Take a seat, girl,' Bast insisted, extending her hand. Cali manoeuvred her avatar to sit in one of the seats.

'To be able to spread the light that Earth so desperately needs, you need to come into alignment. In The Queendom, it's easy to see when you're fully activated, because your whole being will glow. If it was only this easy on Earth! Come, sit. Let me show you. I promise you, it doesn't hurt. Let's plug you into the source,' Bast said excitedly. Cali clicked her mouse and a mask dropped down over her avatar's face. 'Remember, it's as easy as ABC. All you need to do to begin with is breathe. Breathe in deeply. Let your belly rise, then exhale fully and let everything go.' On screen, a sphere of light appeared in the centre of her avatar's chest. It grew brighter as Cali breathed in, and it dimmed as she breathed out, mimicking the rise and fall of her belly. At first, it felt hard to synchronise and match the slow pace, almost as if she didn't have enough space inside her for all the air she inhaled, but after a few minutes, she watched as a glowing, bright, liquid light moved down the silver tubes into her avatar's body.

'Watch as this light fills your body. Breathe it in, so it can enter your every cell. Breathe long and deep, let the light cleanse your mind. Let it wash away any negative thoughts.'

Cali began to feel calm as she matched her avatar's breathing. After a few moments, her onscreen self glowed with light from head to toe.

'When you go to the underworld to meet the Dark Goddess, you have to remain in your light - and that will take more than just effective breathing,' Bast said, moving closer to Cali's avatar. 'You must keep your vibration elevated and your mind clear. You may not believe it, but you're in control of your mind. You can choose your thoughts. We can project what's on your mind onto this screen, so that we can observe your thoughts and train you. But also input positive visualisations' A movie exploded, right in front of Cali's eyes. Hundreds of light warriors, girls just like her, stood in the power pose. She saw a tribe of soul star sisters all celebrating as though they'd accomplished their missions. She felt inspired, strong, powerful and filled with joy. She watched these imagined future moments from the game and felt the energy inside her ignite, to the point where she could have jumped down from the top bunk to do a little dance.

'That's the power of emotion. When we choose to imagine the best outcomes, high vibe emotions are the result. We feel happy and energised, we feel powerful and our auras become strong and full of light. Let the good sensations tingle through your body and spread out into the world, this is energy in motion.'

Cali thought it was spooky that this wasn't just happening to her avatar, but to her, too. As she filled with positive emotions, the light in the game started to spread out from her avatar's body to the furthest corners of the galaxy.

'When you're in flow like this, anything you see in your imagination you can create in The Queendom. It also happens this way on Earth, except most people don't believe it. Say you want to manifest the key, for example...'

Cali's ears pricked up and she thought about how close she'd come to the key at the museum.

'You see it in your mind. Feel the emotions and sensations as though you have it in your hand. Believe it will happen, declare your intention, then release it, trusting that it will appear in divine timing.

You must trust you will manifest the key, that it will come to you in your world. Look out for the signs and synchronicities that the goddesses will send you. '

Cali felt a tinge of envy that she couldn't fully experience the wonderful energy flow, like her onscreen self. She wondered if she'd ever feel that special. Would she ever find the key in real life?

Once doubt crept in, it spread rapidly, contaminating every other thought that surrounded it, ripping up the happy images and injecting a lethal dose of negativity.

'What happens to your state when you're met by darkness? Are you able to honour your emotions? To move forward, regardless of the inner doubt and fear? That's the true work of the Light Warrior.'

Cali's inner voice took on a sharp, critical tone. *'Let's not get carried away. This is, after all, just make believe, a game, i.e. not real. Those other girls might be strong enough to succeed in their missions, but they're all great warriors. Who are you? You're just a pathetic little nobody, or have you forgotten that?'*

Cali froze. Her mind took complete control and began switching to voices that haunted her the most. Suddenly, Poppy's face flashed up on the visor, making her jump out of her skin. Poppy's sarcastic, sickly smile taunted her, and her green eyes glared right at Cali. She backed away from the screen and saw the light retract; it was invaded by a dark, cloudy substance that raced down the tubes.

Bast spoke into a radio. In an instant, Eset's face appeared in a holographic transmission on the wall of the cave.

'You must keep your thoughts pure. Focus on your breathing and clear your mind,' she commanded. 'Some of the worst bullies exist within our own mind. Be kind to yourself.'

Fear already had Cali in its grip. Her thoughts became amplified and projected disaster scenarios in front of her eyes, which only created more panic and anxiety within her, then more darkness. She was trapped in a negative spiral that was sucking out all of her light.

'Disconnect. Disconnect. Your thoughts are contaminated. The shadow has reached your aura,' a strange, mechanical voice interjected. Interference disrupted the transmission and Eset's face disappeared until there was nothing. All the light had gone.

Cali repeatedly pressed the spacebar, but she couldn't get her avatar to move. It was no use. She watched the darkness travel towards her avatar. The tube broke free from the wall and began to flap around the cavern like a possessed snake, her avatar still attached to the other end. It flung it around the cave, rebounded it off the walls and hit it against the ceiling before slamming it onto the floor. The tube finally broke free. Cali watched with horror as her avatar fell in a heap.

The history Lesson
Ch 15

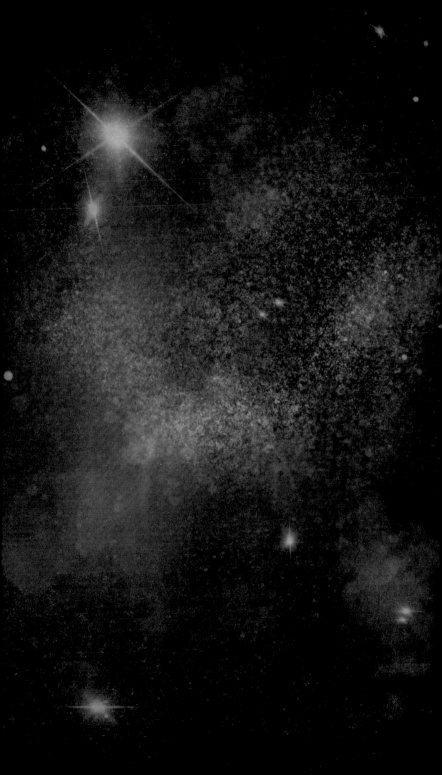

Cali walked down the long, wood-panelled corridor in a zombie-like fashion. She'd stayed up late again, playing the game; afterwards, her sleep had been tormented by her inability to do anything right, and of her wasting every chance she'd been given to find the key. The witch had even found her way into her dreams now. The dark, hollow eyes from her three haunting faces stared deeply into Cali, on many levels. It was like there was no escape from her darkness. She'd woken up, sweating, and gasping for breath.

Her tired eyes failed to register any of the framed black and white photos that lined the walls, of stuffy looking boys standing proudly in uniform - portraits from years gone by, before girls were allowed to attend. She'd once played a game with Zia where they'd attempted to work out which one of the strange-looking loonies had tried to set the school on fire. There was a rumour that arson was the cause when the entire school was destroyed in 1904. Whichever weirdo did it was the reason they had to constantly recite the Latin motto 'Clarior ex Ignibus', which could be read on the school's badge; it meant 'a light forged in fire'. Mr Tenbridge harped on about it at every possible opportunity. That's why they'd chosen the symbol of the legendary phoenix to represent the school, an imaginary bird that burst into flames, only to be reborn from its own ashes.

Cali reached her locker, opened the door and riffled through the books and loose papers inside. Her fingers came across an item she didn't recognise. On the outside was a soft, velvety material, though she could feel something hard encased within. Suddenly, Cali was wide-awake as she pulled the item out.

She opened the box and stumbled backwards in shock. Glistening, in the palm of her hand, was the ankh. Cali looked all around her, but no one was near enough to notice. It was as if the whole world had stood still. She sensed that the ankh had its own powerful energy.

Cali felt butterflies in her chest, an excitable lightness that took her breath away, as thoughts swirled in her head like colorful leaves floating in the autumn breeze.

'Oh my goodness. I can't believe it. It's here. It's actually right here,' she whispered, holding the ankh close to her heart and breathing deeply. She then studied every aspect of its smooth, red crystal, which felt cool to the touch. She pulled its silver chain over her head. Today, she didn't care about school rules. Today, she was going to wear the ankh with pride. 'Thank you, Eset. Now that I finally have the key, I won't let you down. I knew I should have trusted you. You said it would come to me, and here it is.'

Cali went to her first class. Ms Ombassu stood at the front of the room and coughed loudly to silence the chatter. Although she was petite, she had a huge presence, and Cali liked the way she was firm yet fair; she was also impressed by the way she commanded the room with a cough. She realised that Ms Ombassu was smiling right at her. Cali avoided her stare, embarrassed.

'Right, class, following our visit to the museum, we'll be looking deeper into the ancient myths, in honour of one special student.' She looked at Cali and smiled. 'I want to approach this from a different angle today, by examining the role that the global goddess has played in ancient history, and the impact this has had on our culture today.'

Cali couldn't believe what she was hearing. She felt a warm flush spread to her cheeks. Was the ankh working its magic already? She was excited, she hadn't felt this way in months. Finally, her luck was changing. Plus, Poppy wasn't in this lesson, so she could learn all about the goddesses without worrying that it would be thrown back in her face.

'Can anyone tell me what a goddess is and why they're important to women today?'

The class seemed to let out a collective moan. A few of the boys shouted out comments that made Cali sink a little in her seat.

'Goddesses aren't real though, are they, miss?'

'They only exist in myths, in made up stories.'

'Aren't they some kind of underwear model?' one boy mocked.

Ms Ombassu raised her hand to silence their remarks. 'Okay, let's explore this a little deeper. A goddess is a female deity or a representation of the divine feminine. She can be found in religious traditions all over the world: Hinduism, Buddhism, Paganism. The ancient cultures of Greece and Egypt worshipped the goddess. Each goddess has her own unique qualities, talents and rituals. They embody a variety of different archetypes or roles, like warriors, mothers, magicians and lovers.'

Ms Ombassu pointed the remote control at the screen at the front of class and a video showed images of different goddesses. There was Athena, the Greek warrior goddess of wisdom; Pele, the Hawaiian goddess of fire; Shakti, the Hindu goddess of the divine mother; Aphrodite, the goddess of love; Ishtar, the high priestess; Hecate, the wise witch; and, Isis, queen of the heavens. Cali looked at each image and felt deep recognition.

'Does anyone have any comments? Why would these figures appeal to women and girls today?' asked Ms Ombassu, as she paced the classroom.

She stopped in front of Cali. Her presence alone urged her to speak up. 'Well, lately, I've been learning quite a lot about goddesses; not intentionally, to be honest. It's like they found me when I needed them. Does that make sense? The Egyptian one, Eset, I mean Isis, is not what you might think...' Cali hesitated and took a deep breath.

'Please go on,' said Ms Ombassu. 'We'd like to hear your views.'

Cali felt her throat tightening. She didn't like attention, particularly about something so deeply personal. 'To me, the goddess represents a different kind of power that's needed in the world today. A power that, um, needs to be found within each of us. It's like the more feminine qualities that are often seen as weak...like empathy, kindness, compassion, intuition...are actually what the world really needs. The goddess shows us what we're capable of. I believe that, if we can connect to our own power and be guided by something bigger than ourselves, we can make positive changes in the world.'

The whole classroom was quiet and Cali became conscious of her voice. She couldn't remember exactly what she'd just said, or even if it made sense. She worried that she'd said too much.

'That's really wonderful, Cali. What an eloquent and personal account of this subject. Thank you so much for sharing.' Cali felt a warm sensation spread through her body. She felt sure it was the power of the ankh that was making her feel full of potential and possibility.

The class spent the rest of the session looking at myths and debating the history of gods and goddesses. It was the best lesson Cali had ever had. She felt disappointed when the bell rang and wished it could have lasted a little longer.

Cali strode into the corridor with a new sense of self. She felt two feet taller and remembered that the delicate yet powerful crystal in the ankh was a symbol of strength. As she turned the corner, she bumped into Poppy and Martha. They sprang apart like repellent forces

Poppy's bright blue eyes looked Cali up and down with an air of distaste, depicted by the slight flare of her nostrils. Cali held her ground and returned her stare. A smirk crawled across Poppy's lips and a glint of danger flashed in her eyes. She leaned closer and grabbed hold of the ankh, threatening to yank it off its chain.

'Can you believe the nerve of this witch?' she seethed, loudly enough that the hallway traffic stopped. 'Not only has she gone and stolen my precious and very expensive property, she's got the bloody nerve to actually wear it and taunt me with it.'

'What are you talking about? I haven't stolen anything, this was a gift!'

'A gift? Who on earth would give you such an expensive gift?' Poppy was practically shouting now, and Cali was aware that people were watching. 'I don't know when or how you managed to steal my necklace, but the security camera at the shop will clearly show you gawking at it and me buying it.' Poppy was so close that Cali could smell the stale coffee on her breath. 'Oh, darling, you didn't really think it was a gift from the goddesses, did you?' she said, before breaking out into raucous laughter. Martha followed suit.

The colour drained from Cali's face as she realised she'd been set up. It wasn't real. It wasn't the sign she'd been waiting for, it wasn't the key that she needed, it was just a cruel prank. Cali felt like the wind had been knocked right out of her as she searched frantically in her mind for the right lesson, the right wisdom. She found nothing except that critical voice that cursed her for being so stupid. As her mind defaulted to negative outcomes and disaster scenarios, panic began to rise. It bubbled up from her belly; it was like all the lovely butterflies she'd felt in Ms Ombassu's lesson suddenly had wings of concrete. The goddesses had abandoned her.

149

Mothers' Meeting
Ch 16

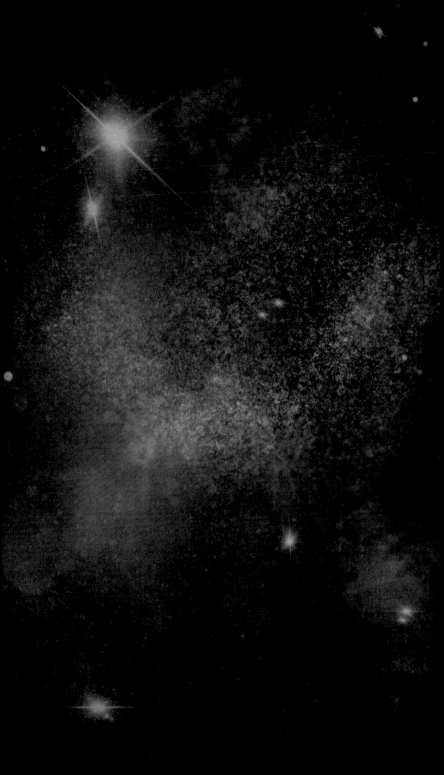

The tick-tock of the tall, wooden grandfather clock in the corner was the only sound in the tiny office. Its background beat seemed deafening amid the heavy silence. Three mothers sat on old, green, leather padded chairs, a small distance apart. Cali, Poppy and Zia stood behind them. They faced the large mahogany desk where Mr Tenbridge, the school principal, sat. He pushed his glasses towards the ridge of his nose and took a deep breath; the action made a slight whistling sound, which always made the students giggle. Cali couldn't help but stare at the wiry hairs protruding from his nostrils. As her gaze travelled up to the wild, grey eyebrows overshadowing his dark eyes, she realised he was staring back at her, scrutinising her with disdain. Cali quickly looked down at her scuffed black shoes, her cheeks flushing.

'I can categorically state that this is not some...witch hunt as you call it,' he said, hesitating before the word 'witch', like it didn't belong in his vocabulary. 'We have credible witnesses that can clearly place Cali in the gift shop looking at the stolen item.'

'Gerard,' Poppy's mum responded, in a soft tone that made Cali and Zia look at each other and stifle a giggle. 'I mean, Mr Tenbridge,' she corrected, shooting the girls a look that could kill. 'I don't think there can be any discussion here, really. This is most definitely a matter for the police. It goes against every principle of the school. Although the publicity will be horrendous, we must abide by our values.'

Mrs Delongue clutched at the pearls around her neck. The gigantic diamond ring on her finger scattered light across the wood-panelled walls.

'Mum, honestly, for the hundredth time, I didn't do it! I did not take the necklace. It was inside my locker when I found it,' insisted Cali. Her eyes felt like they could burn right through her mum's cheek, as she avoided Cali's gaze.

'Hush, Cali, it's okay,' she replied, in an attempt to quiet her. Turning to Mrs Delongue, Cali's mum said, 'Kids these days can often make mistakes. Cali's new here and just trying to fit in. Surely we can work this out between us.'

'Oh, please. I see you're trying very hard, but you're in no position to bargain. We put a lot of effort into upholding our charitable aims for the school; clearly, that's often to our detriment.' She smiled widely, flashing her perfectly aligned, bright white teeth. Cali couldn't help but notice that the smile didn't reach her eyes.

'Hang on a minute, are you trying to say we're some kind of charity case?' Cali could tell her mum was getting angry; her pretend posh voice was starting to slip, and her true northern accent was coming out. 'We pay our bills exactly the same as you do.'

'I appreciate the intention, but for some of us, taking that step above our station does more harm than good.'

'How dare you!' Cali could feel the fire begin to rise within her mother, the same heat that rose within her, the same fire that could become out of control, the exact same power that was just waiting to explode. She studied her mum's face. She could see that she was shaking and trying desperately to hold back tears. 'I work extremely hard to send my daughter to this school.'

'I can see that, my dear, I really can. My family founded this school and has always helped those in need. Yet, this is clearly affecting your mental and emotional wellbeing. No matter how hard you try, it's not going to be sustainable in the long run.'

Zia's mum stood up and moved between the two of them.

'I need to stop this right here. Can we just take a few breaths and calm the situation down?' She was as serene as ever.

Mrs Delongue looked at her with raised eyebrows.

Ms Ombassu continued. 'I was with the girls on the trip, and I know, without a shadow of a doubt, that neither of them have the capacity or the motivation to steal anything. Speaking not just as a mother, but as a teacher, they are both kind and honest girls who have had some challenging confrontations with Poppy in the past.' Zia's mum chose her words carefully.

'Don't you dare suggest that my daughter is somehow to blame. Clearly, you don't value your job.' The air seemed to turn colder and everyone sat on the edge of their seats. Mr Tenbridge fiddled with his tie, looking more awkward than Cali had ever seen him.

'Ladies, I'm sorry, but I have to bring some kind of conclusion to our meeting. I've made my decision based solely on the facts, and the facts are that the stolen item was found in Cali's possession.' He paused to read the spidery handwriting on his desk pad. 'Therefore, I have no option but to suspend Cali Roberts, whilst we work with the museum and the police as part of a full investigation.'

Cali heard her mother take in a sharp breath and she mentally prepared herself for the fallout. She could hardly believe she was hearing these exact words again. It was like some terrible case of déjà vu, like a bad dream that she couldn't wake up from. She looked at her mum's horrified expression, then at Zia's shocked face, then to Poppy's smug smile, and finally to Ms Ombassu, who cleared her throat and broke the heavy silence.

'Mr Tenbridge, I urge you to reconsider. Cali says the necklace had been placed in her locker; therefore, all the other evidence is hearsay.'

'And I,' shouted Mrs Delongue, her nostrils fully flaring as she glared at them with a look of utter disgust, 'urge you, Ms Ombassu, to kindly remember your place.'

Mrs Roberts stood up. She looked a bit dizzy as she

turned to leave. 'Thank you, Mr Tenbridge,' she said.

Cali followed her mum out of the old, red stone building and through the neatly kept gardens; she struggled to keep up with her pace as they marched towards the car park. The path was lined with bushes that held the remnants of soggy, shrivelled roses that threatened to drop their leaves on the ground. Her mother got in the car and slammed the door. Cali climbed in silently.

'Suspended, Cali?' she finally said in utter disbelief. 'Do you realise just how much of a mess you've created, yet again? I don't think I can forgive you for this. Everything I've done, all the sacrifices, all the work, all for bloody nothing…' Tears began to stream down her face and she angrily wiped them away.

'Mum, it's not my fault. I swear I didn't do it.'

'Like you didn't do it the last time your powers 'accidentally' pushed someone down the stairs? Like the last time you got expelled? Not your fault again, Cali? Really? When are you going to take responsibility for your stupid bloody actions and wake up? Your power is not a gift, it's a curse. The kind that wrecks lives. That's all they've ever done.'

'I did not take the necklace. Why don't you believe me? Why do you never believe me? You're too busy trying to be something you're not, trying to keep up with the Joneses, trying to prove you're this high-powered businesswoman. You know what? I hate you. I don't know how you can even call yourself my mother.'

The response that came was the sound of the car's horn. Cali's mum pounded her fists onto the steering wheel and let out an almost primal cry. The combination of the sounds was harrowing. Cali froze. She wished she could take it all back, swallow her words down, into a place so deep they would disappear forever.

Secret Discoveries
Ch 17

Cali's mum suffered a sharp downturn after the school meeting, which resulted in her taking time off work - something Cali was sure she would never forgive her for. Thankfully, Grandma Georgina came to the rescue, and today was the first time Cali had been allowed to leave the house.

Cali stood at the entrance to the barn and peered into the small, smelly pen at the ginger, floppy-fringed alpaca curled up in the corner. There was a sign attached to the metal railings that stated her name was Alice; she was seven years-old and her favourite food was turnips. Cali wondered what kind of life Alice had, locked up all day. She empathised with the alpaca, having spent the last few days staring at her bedroom walls and avoiding her mum's irrational moods, as some kind of punishment for getting suspended.

She hadn't even wanted to come to the stupid farm. She wasn't five anymore, but she wasn't given the choice. It had been non-negotiable, her mum needed space. Cali felt her phone vibrate in her pocket and pulled it out. It was from Zia. *Hey, Cali, how's you today? Just doing our daily check in. Hope you've not died of boredom overnight.*

Cali texted back: *I'm finally out of the house, but only at a farm with my grandma, so still alive... Just! Nothing exciting to report.*

Zia: *I've got news. Poisonous P is bragging about getting you suspended from school. I swear I want to smash her smug little lying face in. And you'll never guess where the charity ball is taking place, only at her bloody mansion.*

Cali added a laughing emoji to her response: *Wow. I wonder what the mansion looks like. Aren't you the tiniest bit curious?*

Zia: *I'd rather eat my own head.* Zia then sent a photo of her opening her mouth wide as though she was going to swallow the entire phone.

'Cali, can't you put that phone away for just a minute? You're addicted to that thing.' Grandma Georgina shook her head and spoke quietly, looking around to see if anyone else was within earshot. Her wavy, brown, jaw-length hair framed the stern features of her face.

Cali bit her tongue and smiled at her.

'Come on, let's get out of this smelly place and take a walk near the field to see if the donkeys are there. You always loved the donkeys when you were a little girl.' She tapped Cali's arm gently. 'We need to get you out amongst nature. Get some fresh air to blow those cobwebs off.'

They walked past the little playground to the edge of the muddy field that held two horses and three tired donkeys. The animals trotted over to greet them, probably hoping for carrots. Cali remembered visiting the farm so many times when they used to come for the weekend from London. This grandma, her country grandma, would insist on getting them outdoors, and spoiling them with sweets and ice cream. At the same time, she was a little distant and reserved. She was so different from her city grandma, Grandma Gracie, who was larger than life and motherly - though you wouldn't dare step out of line, or you'd know about it.

Cali built up the courage to break the silence and ask the question everyone seemed to be avoiding. 'Grandma, do you think Mum's going to be okay?'

'I couldn't tell you, Cali. Your mum won't talk to me,' she replied, suddenly becoming very interested in the donkey in front of her, which was sticking out its tongue and slavering. 'You know it can't be easy for her, what with all that's going on with you at school, and with her job...and, to top it all off, your dad being away for weeks on end.' She shook her head. 'It's hard being a mum, you know. You don't get a manual that tells you how to do it right. Your mum's going through a tough time and she needs some compassion and space for herself to rest.'

Cali felt her anger begin to boil. Funnily enough, she was all out of compassion. In fact, she felt like throwing her sensitive side in the bin. Meeting the goddesses and following her heart had only created more problems and issues in her life.

'What was she like when she was little?'

'History has a way of repeating itself,' Grandma Georgina muttered quietly as she looked into the distance. 'Oh, look at the time! We need to make a move or we won't get back for Eva.'

*

'Hello, I'm home.' Cali's voice rang out into the empty hallway and was greeted with silence. At least Rocco, her cute cockapoo, was excited to see her. The house seemed eerily empty; Eva was at school and her dad had left at the weekend. Cali hadn't been as sad as she usually would be about that. She was truly in his bad books over the latest turn of events. Even though she felt he believed she was telling the truth - unlike her mum, who was obsessed with appearances - she'd lost sight of what was real and what wasn't.

She walked into the kitchen, stepping over clothes, toys and shoes that were strewn all over the floor. She felt relieved that Grandma Georgina had had to rush off to collect Eva from school, as she was sure she would have had a lot to say about the state of the house. Cali opened the door of the big American fridge-freezer and shuddered at the near-empty shelves, bearing only expired yoghurt, hard cheese and mouldy carrots - the juice of which had pooled at the bottom of the pull-out drawer. She hadn't even mentioned to Grandma Georgina that she'd been living on noodles and toast lately.

She bent down to pick up some books and Barbies from the floor and noticed some shattered glass. She piled the toys up on the sideboard and scanned the floor. Just as she was about to shout to her mum from the bottom of the stairs, she noticed the door to the basement was open and the light was on.

The basement was the one part of the house the family didn't venture into, because both the staircase and the electrics were dodgy. Cali was strictly forbidden to go down there.

'MUM?!' Cali shouted into the basement. There was no answer. She felt a shiver run down her spine, it made her feet stick to the top step as if they'd been superglued there. After calling out repeatedly with no response, she figured her mother must be upstairs in her bedroom. Cali dragged her feet up the stairs, Rocco following close at her heels. She peered round the corner of her mum's bedroom door to find the room in darkness; the curtains hadn't been opened and only a sliver of light managed to creep through the gap. It was just enough to highlight her mum's outline. She had her back to Cali, as she laid in the large, king-sized bed, wrapped under the white duvet.

The room was a mess. Large cardboard boxes full of books and paper surrounded the bed and she noticed the musty smell in the air. Cali side-stepped through the debris. She bent down and gently prodded her mum's shoulder, leaning in closer so she could speak into her ear.

'Mum? Are you okay? I'm back now. Mum, can you hear me?' There was no response. She must be in a deep sleep, though Cali. Then she looked over at the bedside table. Bottles of perfume and tubes of face cream covered its mirrored surface, but Cali noticed a medical foil with only a few tablets left. The packaging didn't look like that of the paracetamol in the kitchen cupboard. Cali couldn't pronounce the long name printed on the foil. The thought crossed her mind that maybe her mum was really sick and that was why she'd been acting so weird lately, walking around in a daze.

She watched her mum's chest rise and fall and felt an overwhelming sense of sadness. It was like someone had scooped out all her insides until she was hollow. She had the urge to curl up next to her mum, like she did many years ago. Cali planted a tender kiss on her mum's fingertips and gently brushed them against the side of her cheek, just like she used to do to her.

'It's going to be okay, Mum, I promise you,' she whispered, before turning to leave. Cali took one last glance at the boxes and the papers scattered all over the room. Her mum was not the tidiest person, but this seemed bad, even for her. As she looked closer, she saw the papers were paintings, sketches and pencil drawings. Some were crumpled and torn in two. Most of them contained beautiful, intricate, detailed wings; wings that looked angelic and other-worldly. They reminded Cali of The Queendom, the goddesses, of Eset and the other angelic beings she'd seen.

Why would Mum be drawing things like this? What had she been looking for in the old boxes in the basement? There was still no movement from the bed. Cali approached one of the boxes and sat beside it. Once again, chills ran up her spine, making the hairs on her arms stand to attention.

Inside the box, Cali found old trinkets and souvenirs - postcards from Spain, and a photo of her mum looking radiant, happy and young. She was twirling around in a red dress against a clear, aquamarine sea. Cali could hardly believe it was her mum. She looked so different, so free. Cali delved deeper into the box, a little nervous as to what she might find. She pulled out silk-bound journals filled to the brim with handwritten notes and illustrations. She flicked through the pages, wondering if she should intrude. If her mum woke up, she'd be in even more trouble.

She was about to repack everything when she spotted a wooden box. The lid had delicately-carved turquoise, accented with gold. Just holding it, she could feel an incredible energy emanating; it flowed into her hands and made them tingle. Inside, there was a velvet material that she removed to reveal the most stunning golden ankh with the same three crystals Bast had given her in the crystalline core. A red one, a black shiny one, and a glowing white one. Cali examined the crystals then put them into her pocket.

Is this some kind of joke? she wondered. *The key, after everything I've been through? Here? It was here all along?*

Cali didn't understand what it meant, and she wasn't sure she wanted to find out. At that moment, her mum let out a high-pitched scream. She sat, bolt upright, in the bed. Her forehead was covered in beads of sweat and strands of her hair were stuck to her face.

'Mum, are you okay?' Cali asked, rushing to her side. Her mum looked at Cali as though she didn't recognise her; she then looked around the room, as though she was trying to work out where she was. She seemed completely disorientated.

'It's me, Cali. You've had a bad dream.'

Her mum looked around the bedroom again then stared down at Cali's hands. It took a moment to register the ankh Cali was holding.

'Where did you find that?' she asked, not taking her eyes off it.

'I found it in one of your boxes on the floor,' stuttered Cali. 'You know it's practically the same as the one Poppy planted in my locker. The same one the goddesses in the game showed me. I'm kind of wondering why you have one too,' she whispered.

Her mum looked at Cali. She then put her face in her hands and began to cry. 'There's so much I need to say. I don't know where to start. I never wanted you to see the darkness, I've tried so hard to keep it from you. We're the same, you and me. People like us are not made for a world like this. I've had to deny my power, it's the only way I could survive.' She paused and looked away.

'When I was a little girl, I used to sense and see things that other people didn't...these winged beings and angelic creatures. I didn't know what they were back then, it wasn't until much later I came to realise they were goddesses.'

As Cali heard those words from her mum's mouth, she felt a shiver down her spine. She couldn't believe what she was hearing.

'They made me feel like I wasn't quite so alone. One day, I asked my mum about the 'visitors', but she got so angry with me. 'We don't believe in those kinds of things in this house,' Grandma would say. She took me to doctors and psychologists, who ran tests and studied me. They said my fear of the dark was irrational, and I was just told to stop making things up. They all agreed that I had an overactive imagination and it was simply episodes of attention seeking behaviour. Any time I mentioned it after that, I was punished for believing in the unseen world, and taught to suppress my powers. I was locked in my tiny room in the darkness and left alone to cry myself to sleep.'

Cali's mum then pulled her knees up to her chest and hugged herself tightly. She looked like a lost little girl as her back heaved and sobs escaped into the room.

Cali sat perfectly still, hoping that, if she didn't

move, she might disappear completely. Her mind grasped for a solution - the right thing to say or do to make it all better.

'You know, when you were little, Cali, if I was ever sad, you used to point at my paintings and say, 'The angel lady says she loves you, Mummy, you're not alone.' It used to make me feel like it was you and me against the world. How did I lose my way so badly?'

Cali had no idea how to answer and she wasn't sure her mum really wanted her to, anyway. Her mind spun, trying to rewind, pause, go back in time, and find those moments with her mum. To hear, once again, her words, that told Cali they were more alike than she could have ever imagined. That her mum had powers, just like she had, and that she knew about the other world Cali was only just discovering.

Cali looked at her mum and sensed a real sadness and regret in her, like she'd truly lost her way and was miles from anything she could call home.

'Mum, it's going to be okay,' was all Cali could muster, though she suspected her attempt to reassure her mother wasn't very convincing.

The Witch
Ch 18

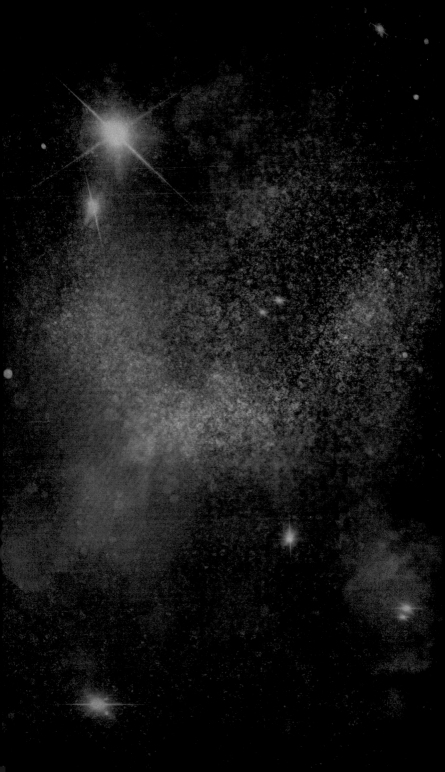

'We're home!' Grandma Georgina shouted. Cali gave her mum's hand a squeeze, welcoming the excuse to leave the uncomfortable atmosphere in the bedroom to greet them.

Eva's face and hands were covered in glitter. She proudly waved a handmade card in the air. 'I made a card for Mummy, I want to show it to her,' Eva squealed, wriggling out of her grandma's arms and rushing towards the stairs.

'Not so fast, Eva, Mummy's still sleeping.' Cali reached down to hug her sister a little more tightly than she normally would, breathing in the smell of plasticine and glue.

'Eva, it's so beautiful, why don't you show it to your sister?' said Grandma Georgina. 'I know your mummy will love it just as much when she wakes up. You really are a fabulous artist, just like her.'

'I know, Grandma. I'm the best in my class,' Eva answered, which made them both laugh.

Grandma Georgina looked around the kitchen. She pushed up the sleeves of her sweater and began clearing all the dirty cups and plates. She opened the glass doors that led to the garden. The birds could be heard chirping away as the sun set over the trees. 'Why don't you girls play while I make us a lovely dinner? I bought your favourite food,' she said, grabbing the carrier bags from the floor. 'Spaghetti Bolognese and garlic bread with cheese.'

Cali would have normally retreated to her room, but her grandma's presence felt comforting. She chased her little sister outside, Rocco barking excitedly at their heels. They ran to the far end of the garden and the rope swing their dad had made. It had a wonky wooden seat and was attached to the branches of the old apple tree; it was currently surrounded by the last few apples to fall. The ones on the floor were brown and rotting.

169

Eva's giggles got louder with each push, as she climbed higher and higher in the crisp evening air. Cali kicked off her fluffy bunny slippers and let her bare feet sink into the cold, mossy grass. For a moment, she imagined she had roots attached to the bottom of her feet, which travelled deep into the earth, just like the Tree of Life. With each breath, she felt like she was sending all her worries into the earth. Worries about her mum, about Poppy, about school, and facing the Dark Goddess; she sent these deep into the soil and imagined that, in return, the earth was sending nourishing energy to soothe her system. Cali wasn't sure if it was her imagination, but she felt her mind becoming a little clearer; her thoughts, a little calmer; her breathing, a little deeper. Maybe she was going to be okay, after all.

Grandma Georgina called them back in and Cali laid the table, which she'd done whenever they'd had guests at their old house. Dinner was delicious. She was surprised at how quickly she managed to clear her plate, she even wiped up some of the sauce with garlic bread. Eva sucked up the spaghetti so enthusiastically it turned her chin orange. After they'd finished, their dad called to check in. After a long conversation with Grandma Georgina, he came back on to say bye, and promised to bring lots of sweets with him when he returned.

Once the table was cleared and the dishes washed, they all sat together on the sofa with fluffy blankets and selected a movie. It was one Cali had watched a hundred times before. She found it hard to concentrate, as she couldn't help thinking about the ankh amongst her mother's things and also something her grandma said to her at the farm. She pretended to be engrossed in the film while thinking of how she could build up the courage to ask Grandma Georgina about it. Finally, Eva fell fast asleep, with her head in Grandma Georgina's lap.

Cali blurted the words out. 'Grandma, you said something before about history repeating itself. I wondered if you knew something about mum's fear of the dark and her nightmares.'

Grandma Georgina stroked Eva's hair and looked directly at Cali. 'I've been waiting for the day where you would ask me this.' She reached out to take Cali's hands in hers. Then, taking a deep breath, she said, 'For generations, the women in our family have been haunted by the Dark Goddess. It's an unspoken secret.' In that moment, Cali felt like her whole world had come to a standstill. It was as if all of her 'spidey' sensors had been switched up to their highest level of sensitivity. She listened as her grandma spoke. It was as if two worlds were colliding - the world of the game and the real world.

'I've made mistakes, Cali, none of us have managed to get it right - not my mother, or my mother's mother. There's been too much pain associated with our powers. So, we all learnt to deny, avoid and suppress them. Only now am I realising the real cost of that.'

Cali took a deep breath. She felt the shock of each new sentence like a blow to the belly and wondered if she dared even mention what she'd found earlier.

'Grandma, today I found the ankh in an old box in Mum's room.'

Her grandma went pale and looked away. 'Well, it looks like the key has found you this time. Maybe you're the one who can finally make things alright.' She smiled meekly at Cali then stroked the side of Eva's face. 'Right, I best get your sister to bed, it's getting late.'

At that moment, Cali felt her phone vibrate. She pulled it out of her pocket to see a message from The Queendom.

'Eset awaits. It's time for your mission. The descent

into the underworld.'

Cali felt a surge of excitement. Maybe she was the one. Maybe it was time for her to finally face her fears. She yawned and excused herself. Once in her room, she pulled out her laptop from under the pillow and clicked on the icon for the game. Eset appeared on screen, her head covered by a light violet cloak, standing by the Tree of Life. Cali instructed her hyper-real avatar to walk towards her. Her daughter, Bast, was in goddess form and stood by her side.

'Welcome back. It's time for your mission, and for you to finally come face to face with the Dark Goddess - Hecate, Queen of the Underworld, her Highness of the Night, Goddess of the Witches.' Eset stroked the bark of the tree gently as she spoke.

'I still don't understand why I have to face that scary, evil looking witch, or how I'm ever going to get a hold of one of her keys,' Cali typed.

'The witch is not what you have been led to believe. You've been conditioned to fear her. You've been fed horror stories about her since your birth, since your mother's, mother's birth. Even the word *witch* is misused and misunderstood,' Eset stated. Images of stereotypical witches filled the screen. 'The word actually means to bend or shape reality. The witch is the healer, the mystic. She was so powerful that she was demonised.' Cali looked at the screen, confused but intrigued.

'It's not that long ago that there was a real fear in women that they might be accused of witchcraft. They were hunted, tortured and burned at the stake. They made women turn against each other to save their children.' Cali shuddered. She wondered if it was really true and why she'd never heard of it before.

'A word of advice before you meet her once more. An aspect of the witch exists within us all. You could say she's our dark mother. Magic and power come at a cost, so be ready to overcome and release your fears - for that's the only way you'll have any chance of gaining the key.' Eset paused and reached out for Cali's avatar's hands. 'Bast will accompany you to the underworld. Are you ready, sister?'

'Yes, I'm ready. Let's do this,' Cali replied, in a voice that didn't sound quite as convincing as she'd hoped it would.

Cali pulled on her headset to better play the game. She switched her view so that she could see through the eyes of her avatar. The sound and the scenes on screen pulled her deeply into the other world. Bast stood beside her; they both reached out their hands to touch the Tree of Life and ask for permission to enter. As they blessed the tree with prayers and gave gratitude, the face of the tree spirit appeared, etched into the ridges of the bark. The tree smiled at them as they waited for the rings in its trunk to expand and create an opening.

Once inside the tree, the screen went dark until bright red roots, like tendrils, appeared from the base of their feet, drawing them down into the depths of the earth. They seemed to travel faster and further than they did the first time, travelling down, deeper and deeper, until they reached Earth's core. Cali heard the slow, steady beat of a drum; it sounded like a heartbeat. When the drum stopped, Cali realised they'd arrived. They were in a barren landscape, standing in the moonlight beside a mountain. Bast had shapeshifted back into cat form.

'Now, girl, it's time. You must approach the cave of Hecate,' Bast purred, rubbing her body against Cali's avatar's legs. 'I'm going to have to get all serious with you now. We're at the inner sanctum that is the womb of Mother Earth.

Repeat after me: *Queen of the Night, Goddess of the Witches, I enter the darkness seeking the key that opens both the inner and outer realms.'*

Cali whispered the words to the screen.

'Walk forward into the cave. There are torches that will light the way. When you finally come face to face with Hecate, you must transmute her energy and claim your key. Remember, your power is in your presence.' Bast opened her incredible turquoise wings at the mouth of the cave. 'I must leave you here, I cannot walk with you any further.'

Cali felt exposed and alone. She made her avatar clutch the pouch containing the crystals to its chest. She followed the torchlights that dimly lit the stony walls deep into the belly of the cave, until she reached a space with black, rounded walls, glistening with crystals. There she stood, the Dark Goddess, Hecate, next to a huge, black iron cauldron that hissed and spat upon a flaming fire. Draped in dark velvet, the pale skin of Hecate's three faces glowed like moonlight, framed by her long, dark hair. Her eyes were like deep pools of black oil. The long, delicate fingers of her six hands grasped the air, gesturing to Cali to cross the threshold and come closer.

'Welcome to the underworld. You should be proud that you've made it to the inner sanctum.'

Cali felt like her blood had left her body. Her breath became shallow and her pupils dilated, as she became transfixed to the scene before her.

'Do not fear me. The darkness does not exist to scare, it's a part of the natural cycles of birth, death and rebirth.' Hecate reached into her pockets and brought out a pack of cards. She shuffled them and pulled a card that bore an image of a man who was dangling upside down by his ankle. Below the image were the words 'The Hanged Man'. She smiled knowingly. 'Bring me your offering. What are you ready to release? What thought, what belief, what is preventing you from stepping into your power?'

Cali's avatar reached for the releasing stone from

Hecate

the pouch and held it to its heart. Cali followed the ritual. She could hear Eset's words in her mind, 'It's as easy as ABC. Activate your awareness, anchor into your body and breathe, and when you're calm, you can connect with clarity.' Cali brought her palms together at her heart. Her breath slowed and she felt all her senses switch on. She imagined a ball of light surrounding her and repeated the mantra three times. 'I am safe, I am connected and protected. I'm not alone.'

Cali began to feel tingly in real life, in the presence of the Dark Goddess. She resisted any urges to look away or shut her laptop. At that moment, Rocco came into the bedroom, making Cali jump. He ran around the room, growling. Cali knew he sensed the energy of the Dark Goddess, too.

'I think I need to let go of my need to fit in,' Cali answered.

'Yes! I can sense a lot of fear within, fear of being your true self. Until you confront the fears and the stereotypes the word witch evokes, you won't be able to access the power she possesses,' Hecate declared as fire rose from the cauldron. 'You're rejecting your power with this obsession of being liked, being a good girl, and holding in your truth, so as not to upset others. A part of you is dying inside when you say yes, even though your soul is screaming no.'
Cali felt the truth of each word sting. She never realised that hiding parts of herself was stealing her life force.

'You don't need to conform. When you try to be something you're not, you reject yourself, and your powers erupt in anger to cause devastation around you. The witch is the rebel in you. It's time to be yourself. Are you ready to give me your offering and release all of that?'

Cali nodded. Her avatar pulled out the dark crystal from the pouch.

'Allow yourself to feel the emotions and give them to the crystal, to transmute and transform.'

Cali selected the word *fear* from the list of negative emotions that had appeared above her, then watched as her avatar held the crystal to its lips and blew. Dark images appeared in the heart and moved through her avatar's body, streaming out of its mouth in thick, black smoke, which was absorbed by the crystal. As she watched, Cali imagined she was blowing all of her fears away. Her fears of not fitting in, being exposed, ridiculed, hurt and abandoned.

'That's right, release all limitations. Release what no longer serves you. You cannot enter the garden until you've released the heaviness that weighs you down.'

As Cali's avatar finished blowing her fears into the stone, the energy ball around it glowed brighter, lighting up the inside of the cave.

'Everything that makes you fearful is here to help you grow and evolve. Have the courage to face them, to own and cherish all aspects of you. We are more similar than you might believe. I know the injustice you feel, I know what it's like to be the outsider. Now, throw the crystal into the cauldron,' Hecate ordered.

Cali obeyed and had her avatar throw the stone. As it landed in the cauldron, there was fizzing, hissing and popping as a violet flame rose.

'Make peace with me,' Hecate continued. 'For, in accepting me, you accept yourself. You are the magician, the wild one, the healer, the rebel. You are me and I am you. The only way out is to go within. Expand the light ball now, let it grow bigger and brighter.'

Cali watched as the light ball around her avatar got bigger and bigger until it covered Hecate and filled the entire cave. The sight on screen was magical. The light seemed to pulse and illuminate each corner of her bedroom.

'With this key I give to you my power, my magic

and mystery. It's yours, it always was. The witch's most incredible power is her ability to envision and create what she desires, to bend and shift space and time.' Hecate held out the hand with the key. As Cali instructed her avatar to touch it, the screen went blank and was filled with a white glow. Cali could hear the faint ticking of a clock that suddenly slowed until it stopped altogether.

'Hold your focus. Keep your mind clear. You're doing so well. Your power is in your presence. In this moment, we have transcended time. Now, connect to your vision. Imagine the most beautiful, luscious green garden. It's time to step inside.'

Cali closed her eyes and imagined the garden. When she opened her eyes she saw her avatar and Hecate standing in the most idyllic, serene space, surrounded by wildflowers of all sizes and colours. There was soft, green grass below them, a clear blue sky above them. The plants and flowers blew gently in the breeze, dancing and twirling like little fairies to the musical songs of the brightly coloured love birds. The whole place seemed alive with a pure, vibrant, loving energy, like they were all welcoming her home. Cali felt safe. She felt calm inside her mind and body. This is what she imagined it felt like to belong. Hecate approached Cali's avatar and held her in a warm embrace.

'By being brave enough to embrace your shadow and feel safe in the darkness, you're beginning to unlock more of your gifts to see the unseen world. You are a part of it all. Never alone. You can return to your own inner cave and cross through to this garden any time you desire. Just close your eyes, cut off all distractions from the outside, and journey deep into yourself.'

The screen then filled with the image of a golden ankh, a vibrant red crystal at its centre. Eset, Bast and Hecate appeared, making the shape of a triangle around her, and light began to stream from each of their bodies until it filled the entire screen with such brightness that Cali felt she needed sunglasses.

'Congratulations! By taking this first step to embrace and integrate your shadow, you have unlocked the red vortex and illuminated the first step on the rainbow bridge closest to Earth,' Eset declared as the trio of goddesses held hands above their heads. Shooting stars exploded all around them. She'd done it.

The persistent vibration of her phone cut the celebrations short and brought her back to the real world.

Zia: *OMG, OMG, OMG*

Zia: *I've got the most amazing news.*

Zia: *It's GAME OVER.*

Zia: *Cali!!!*

Zia: *Answer me!!!!*

Cali: *What is it? Tell me.*

Zia: *There you are!*

Zia: *Poppy is busted.*

Zia: *My mum managed to get hold of the school security cam, and Poppy can be seen putting the necklace in your locker. You're officially in the clear!*

Cali felt her heart beat loudly and butterflies flutter in her belly. She couldn't believe what she was reading. Could things be starting to turn around? Could this whole nightmare finally be over? Cali wondered if she should wake her mum to tell her, but decided Grandma was probably right to just let her rest.

Cali: *Wow, I can't believe it. I'm so grateful to your mum.*

Zia: *I'm just happy that your crazy butt will be back in school!*

Cali: *Ha! You can't get rid of me that easily.*

Back to School

Ch 19

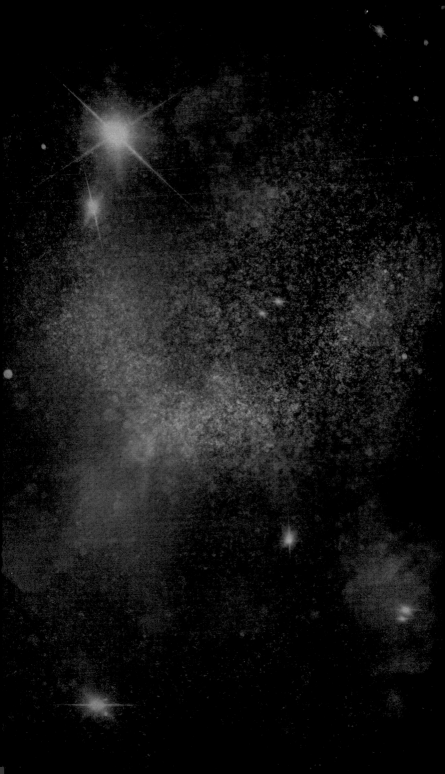

$\mathfrak{C}$ali climbed the five familiar concrete steps and paused at the entrance to the school. Her hand rested on the cold brass handle of the elaborately carved wooden door, and inhaled deeply. It had been two weeks since she'd last stepped through the front door of Crestview School, and she had to admit she hadn't missed it one bit. She felt her mum's hand on her shoulder, gently guiding her forward and finally exhaled. She was returning as quite a different version of herself, compared to the broken, defeated Cali who had walked out of there.

She pushed open the heavy door and walked down the corridor. The glaring strip lights up above were turned off and light from the stained-glass window streamed in, bringing a soft glow to the walls. She glanced at her mum, who was staring ahead with a look of determination. She'd definitely dressed the part. She wore a navy, fitted suit jacket that accentuated her tiny waist, long flowing trousers that swished as she strode down the corridor, and heels that clacked on the black and white tiled floor. Cali was just relieved to finally see her out of her dressing gown.

They turned left at the end of the corridor into the thick, carpeted waiting room. Sat on one of the plaid, padded armchairs in the far corner of the room near the window was Zia and her mum. They both smiled warmly and Zia jumped out of her seat to give Cali a slightly suffocating hug. They were just about to speak when the school secretary, who had a harsh, short bob that matched her temperament, looked them both up and down with an expression of disapproval. 'Ladies, Mr Tenbridge will see you now.'

They entered the headmaster's office to see Poppy and her mother already seated. Mrs Delongue was dressed head to toe in black, as though she were attending a funeral. She clutched a shiny, patent

Birkin bag on her lap, like it was some kind of body shield. Her lips were tightly pursed; she did not look at any of them as they entered and took their seats, which had been strategically placed at the other side of the room.

'Ms Ombassu. Mrs Roberts,' Mr Tenbridge muttered, nodding his head in their direction. 'Well, hello, Cali, and welcome back to Crestview.' His voice had a forced cheerfulness to it, which no one responded to. He cleared his throat to fill the silence, the way he did when everyone failed to laugh at his terrible political jokes in assembly.

'So, firstly, thank you all for attending this meeting. I wanted to come together once again to resolve this issue, so that we can all put this undesirable incident behind us.' He looked at Poppy and raised his eyebrows. 'Poppy has expressed her deep regret to me over this whole unfortunate misunderstanding. And she has something she would like to say to you, Cali.'

Poppy reluctantly got to her feet and looked down at the carpet whilst holding her hands behind her back. She lifted her head to look at Mr Tenbridge, then turned, for the first time, to look tentatively at Cali, with tears brimming in her blue eyes.

'Cali, I'm truly sorry for any hurt my actions may have caused you. I take full responsibility for my behaviour and I want to apologise. I just hope that, in time, you'll be able to forgive me.'

Cali felt anger building within. It began in her belly and rose rapidly up her chest, threatening to burn everything in sight, if it made it out of her body. She turned to look at her mum for some kind of validation, and silently urged her to stand up and speak out on her behalf, but she just sat there, smiling meekly in Mrs Delongue's direction.

Ms Ombassu finally spoke. Her voice cut through the heavy atmosphere in the stuffy office. 'I do not think it's appropriate for this incident to be brushed under the carpet, with fake tears and a polished apology.'

Cali heard both Mr Tenbridge and Poppy's mum take a sharp intake of breath as they braced themselves. She also noticed that her mother was now sitting on the edge of her seat. Cali cursed herself for expecting anything different; her mum always avoided any kind of confrontation.

'After all, we're 'lucky' that I actually managed to get hold of 'that' footage Mr Tenbridge' Ms Ombassu paused, staring directly at the Headmaster. 'I would even go as far as saying that what we have here is a clear case of racial profiling.'

'Oh, Ms Ombassu, I can absolutely assure you that is not the case,' said Mr Tenbridge, rather defensively. Cali looked up admiringly at Zia's mum and wished that her own mother could have just one ounce of her courage and confidence to stand for what was right.

'Well, please do correct my interpretation of this incident, but when Cali was wrongly accused of stealing from Poppy, she was presumed guilty, the police were informed, and she was suspended with immediate effect. So, I don't think it appropriate that the governor's daughter, no less, be excused from such a vindictive act, without any further inquiry or repercussions.'

'Ms Ombassu, have you quite finished?' Poppy's mum interjected. 'I'm sorry, but it appears that you have some kind of personal vendetta against my daughter. You have, time and time again, singled her out. I do not accept these unfounded accusations and find it preposterous that, as an employee of this prestigious school, you could form such a divisive opinion.' Mrs Delongue's face became redder and redder. Cali imagined it exploding like a squashed tomato, splattering its insides across the walls, which made her release a nervous laugh.

'Excuse me, do you find the dragging of my daughter and this school through the dirt amusing?' Mrs Delongue remarked, looking angrily at Cali before bursting into tears.

'Ladies, please,' Mr Tenbridge shouted. He cleared his throat again in an attempt to drown out the sound of everyone talking over each other. 'I assure you that Poppy has been reprimanded, and this incident has been noted on her record. We're here to find resolution, not to create more division.'

Mrs Delongue rummaged inside her bag for a tissue and Poppy uncomfortably shifted from one foot to the other. 'Actually, I wanted to extend a gesture of goodwill, a value this very school is founded on. I would like Cali to join us at our home for the charity ball.' Mrs Delongue dabbed the corners of her eyes whilst looking directly at Cali's mum. 'Please accept this invitation as a white flag, as a way for us to build a bridge and forge a better relationship between our daughters.'

Cali felt the familiar fire rise once again, urging her to rebel - to stand up, to speak out. Hecate's blood was boiling and coursing through her veins. She was angry. Cali was angry, yet there was a blockage. Cali looked at her mum's face and was met with a stony, vacant stare. Mrs Roberts wasn't angry - in fact, she didn't feel anything at all. She just stood there, frozen, devoid of emotion, closed off. Subdued under the external pressure of how she should behave and what was acceptable to say. Cali could see that her mum's energy had already smoothed over the conflict, tucked it away, wrapped it up, and pretended it wasn't happening.

Cali quickly focused her attention on her breathing. She wrapped the light ball around her and repeated the mantra over and over inside her mind.

Cali's mum eventually spoke. 'Well, Mrs Delongue,

I don't want to minimise what Cali...indeed, what we have all been through this last week. It's been an exceptionally difficult time, but I'm also keen to put all of this behind us. That sounds like a kind gesture. Cali would be happy to attend.'

Cali looked at her mum. Her eyes pleaded with her to actually have her back, but her mum was completely oblivious. As Cali looked over at Zia, she saw confirmation of her pain and compassion about the situation reflected in just one look.

'Please call me Penelope,' said Mrs Delongue, shooting a sly look in Ms Ombassu's direction. 'I'm so happy you and I are on the same page.'

The headmaster smiled and clapped his hands together. 'Wonderful! So, now the apology has been accepted, I think we can conclude this meeting. I'm glad we could reach an agreement and make a clean start.' He stood to usher them out of his office, a look of relief on his face.

The mothers and their daughters left the office in single file, and in complete silence. But even if she couldn't see it, Cali could sense unsaid words hanging heavily above them, caught in their auras. The torment, the betrayal, the anger, the injustice, the pain, the guilt, the pride, the embarrassment. Each emotion, stuck there to fester and create a harsh rip in the light. Cali wondered if there could ever be enough dark crystals in the world to absorb it all.

Handbags and Make-up
Ch 20

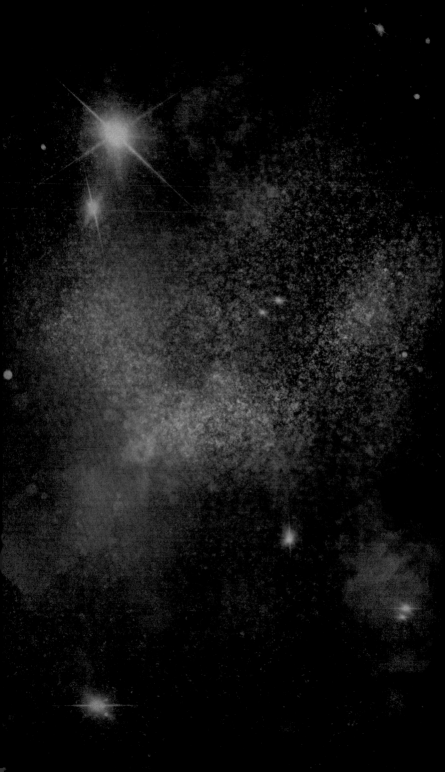

3ia: *Seriously, are you kidding me? Please tell me that you did not fall for that? Going to her house to get ready? Are you crazy? Your mum threw you under the bus and, well, now…you might as well just stick your head in the lion's mouth.*

Cali: *I know, but it's complicated. My mum's not well and I don't want to add to her stress right now. Anyway, Poppy has to be on her best behaviour, now, right?*

Zia: *I wouldn't count on it. Just be careful, newbie. I'm not liking the sound of this. I'll be there as soon as I can, okay?*

Cali: *Don't worry, I've come face to face with worse things. I'm sure I can handle her.*

*

For most of the journey, there was an awkward silence. Cali was becoming very familiar with awkward silences since the meeting at school. Her mum refused to discuss her complete inability to stand up for her, and she still hadn't returned to work. She just retreated into her dressing gown, twenty-four/seven, like it was some kind of comfort blanket.

The sat-nav instructed them to turn off the main road and into a long, gravel driveway surrounded by high fences. As the house came into view, they both gasped. It was a huge, white building, with massive windows and perfectly-manicured gardens.

'Oh, wow, this really is something else. Are you sure you don't want me to walk you to the door?' her mum asked. Cali knew she desperately wanted to be nosy and see inside for herself, so she could compare it with what she lacked, and how she failed to measure up. Cali knew she wouldn't be able to handle it, and she also wanted to avoid any further confrontation with Poppy's mum. She sensed that, on her own turf, Mrs Delongue could be even more vicious.

'No, Mum, it's fine.'

'Now, Cali, I'm sure they're going to take good care of you, but any sign of trouble, you just call me and I'll be back in a jiffy. Okay?'

Cali nodded, grabbed her bag and jumped out of the car before her mum changed her mind. 'Don't forget that Zia's mum is going to be there, and that she'll bring me home. So, don't worry about it, okay?'

As Cali approached the towering front door a spotlight came on automatically, lighting up the plush green bushes that were pruned into perfect spheres in shiny, silver pots. Cali stood centre stage between them, tugging nervously at her hair. She suddenly felt self-conscious; why had she let Zia convince her that she should wear it out? Her fingers pulled on the tight curls as she tried to extend them to full length. Inevitably, frustration followed, as they sprang back the second she let go. On the steps of the mansion, there was no getting away from it - it was the biggest house she'd ever seen in Yorkshire. She turned to wave to her mum, who made a phone shape with her hand and mouthed the words, 'Call me.'

The door was opened by a short, dark-haired lady, whose curves struggled to be contained by the tiny floral apron wrapped tightly around her. Cali instantly recognised her from the 'doll' video as Poppy's nanny.

'Welcome, lovely,' she smiled wearily. 'You must be one of Poppy's school friends. Come in and let me take your coat. I'll show you through.'

Cali followed her through the large, white hallway that was sparkling clean and clear of clutter, and which had a rich, soft vanilla aroma. It was a complete contrast to their untidy home, with walls smeared with slime and a smell of damp dog. Cali noticed little rainbow lights scattered across the walls, reflected by the obnoxiously-huge sparkling chandelier that hung from the ceiling. They passed a large, ornate silver mirror mounted above a table that bore a display of little white orchids in a wide glass bowl. It felt less like a home and more like the fancy hotel they'd stayed in once, when invited to a wedding. Cali caught her rainbow-highlighted reflection in the mirror and watched how her usual worrying thoughts - that she definitely did not belong - were replaced by a stronger sense of self. The girl in the mirror had a bright, shining light surrounding her. Cali was instantly reminded that she was not alone.

The nanny took her up a cream, carpeted grand staircase, then down a wide corridor filled with white flowers, to Poppy's room. It must have been five times the size of Cali's tiny bedroom. It had white walls and an enormous four-poster bed, which had silky, pale-pink bedding with coordinated, plump pillows and cushions.

Poppy owned every kind of toy and gadget you could imagine. Cali felt like she was walking into Harrods' toy department, as she was met by a life-sized, stuffed giraffe that she remembered throwing her arms around as a little girl and refusing to let go of when she saw it in the shop. Poppy was sitting with her legs folded in an orange perspex egg chair, which she spun around to greet her, a wide grin on her face.

'Well, well, well, Cali Roberts, welcome to my home. I have to say, I don't think either of us ever thought we'd see the day that you were actually here in my bedroom.'

The two girls were back in their familiar stance. For a moment, Cali wondered how on earth she'd got herself in such a situation after everything that had happened. Poppy's surroundings just added to her sense of superiority; she used her wealth and entitlement like a shield. It made Cali feel like she didn't measure up, and that she probably never would. She tried to shake off her feelings of unease, but they stuck to her.

'You have to admit, it feels kind of weird,' Cali replied.

'Christine, bring Cali a drink,' Poppy ordered, not even looking in the nanny's direction. Cali was sure she'd got her name wrong - she recalled it was Emily from the video. 'You've got to try one of the mocktails. Mama hired a whole bar with bartenders that juggle glasses with fire and sparklers. They make the best virgin mojitos you've ever tasted.'

Cali couldn't quite muster a smile. Inside, swirled a confusing mixture of intrigue and apprehension, tinged with a sprinkling of unavoidable jealousy. *Who wouldn't want to live in Poppy's world?* It was like looking at the lives of all her favourite YouTubers, who loved to give tours and show off their fancy houses.

'Come on, let's get ready. We've only got an hour before the rest of the school arrives,' Poppy said, jumping up. She walked to a door that opened into a huge, walk-in wardrobe, fitted with rails that were full of clothes, and racks of shoes, stacked neatly by colour. This led through to a private en-suite bathroom with a double sink, a sunken bath and a large flatscreen TV mounted on the wall.

'Wow,' said Cali. She paused before a white shelf, filled with handbags. 'How many of these do you actually have?'

'I've no idea. My parents tend to give me the most expensive ones when they miss my birthday, due to business. The bigger the guilt trip, the better the present!' she laughed.

'You mean your mum has missed your actual

birthday?'

'Oh, God, yeah. Her and Papa have been abroad for six of them so far. I've spent two Christmases with just my nanny and the housekeeper,' Poppy said in a dull tone. 'Mama makes it very clear that business comes first, and that sacrifices have to be made to be able to live the kind of life we live.'

Cali looked at Poppy and saw the little girl inside who knew all too well what it felt like to be overlooked and abandoned. Just as she did. Her head reeled with questions that seemed inappropriate, but which she couldn't stop spilling out of her mouth.

'That's harsh. Doesn't it upset you? I mean, don't you find that hard?'

'Why would I?' responded Poppy, genuinely confused. She began to get undressed, as though Cali wasn't even in the room. 'Why not try something on? Just for fun.'

Cali watched her rummage through the wardrobe and looked at her wistfully. In her mind Poppy had what she thought was a perfect, model-like body - long slim legs, wide, sharp shoulders and a washboard stomach. She wore the most gorgeous white underwear set, which made her tan glow. Poppy finally pulled out some items on gold coat hangers and dangled them in front of Cali's face. 'I've got this amazing Prada dress that's going to look so cute on you. I got it when I did my last modelling job...or maybe this Gucci skirt?' She held up a mini skirt that Cali had seen across social media, worn by all the popular influencers. 'Come on, just try it.' Poppy pulled a pouty face.

Cali eyed it up and down and couldn't resist the thought of actually wearing 'the' skirt that everyone wanted. She pulled her t-shirt up over her head, took off her jeans, and stood awkwardly in her uncoordinated bra and knickers in the centre of the room. She prayed that the crystals she'd shoved in her bra couldn't be seen. She felt exposed and wished there was a way to escape her reflection in the spot-lit mirrors surrounding her.

'Wow! You have the most amazing body. I mean, you are hot! Look at you!'

Cali giggled nervously. 'No, seriously, I don't. I'm not...I mean, I have thick thighs and way too much body hair to be hot,' Cali answered.

'No way, you look incredible. Let's take a selfie, it'll be cute!'

'No, no way. Let's not. Please,' said Cali. 'I can't think of anything worse.'

Poppy had already whipped out her phone and was perfecting her best model pose with a matching pout. She snapped away, giggling, as Cali tried desperately to cover herself with her hands.

'It's okay, I promise I'll keep it safe. It's not like there's anyone at school you'd be bothered about if they saw it, is there?' she asked, raising an eyebrow.

'No. I'm not interested in boys right now. Doesn't seem much point, to be honest.'

'Correct me if I'm wrong, but I'm sure I caught a little moment the other day between you and Nate.'

Cali suddenly felt her cheeks flush and she tried to turn away discreetly.

'I saw the way he looked at you. I'm sure he likes you,' Poppy teased, smiling as she saw Cali's discomfort grow. 'Anyway, try on the skirt. I can't wait to see it on you.' She thrust it into Cali's hands.

Cali felt relieved at the change of subject. 'I'm just worried that it might not fit. I mean, look at you, you're like model thin, and I'm not sure I won't rip it.'

'Oh, stop. Of course it will fit. Come on, I insist.'

Cali pulled on the short denim skirt. Although it was a bit of a squeeze, she managed to get the zip up. She would just have to remember not to sit down or breathe. As she admired her four selves looking back at her from the mirrors, she thought it was worth the risk.

'Help yourself to make-up. You'll find palettes here, and a selection of brushes here,' Poppy said, pointing to where they were kept. 'Do you want me to do your eye make-up for you? You're so pretty, you know, so exotic looking, and your hair is just amazing. Can I touch it?' Poppy asked, reaching out without waiting for permission.

'I'd rather that you didn't,' replied Cali, moving her head to avoid the unwelcome touch.

'Okay then.' Poppy looked slightly insulted and annoyed.

Poppy's mum walked into the room then, shouting into her phone. 'You can't expect me to believe that! It's just not good enough, it all has to be re-done.' She smiled at Cali mid-sentence then twirled her fingers in a circular gesture, as an instruction for Poppy to turn around, as though she needed to inspect her.

'Just a minute.' Mrs Delongue put her hand over the mouthpiece. 'I thought we agreed you were wearing the Prada, darling. The cream is a little unforgiving on you. We've talked about this. You've gained a few pounds from summer. Nobody to blame but yourself. It's definitely got to be the black, it looks much better on you.' She turned to Cali and her eyes bulged as she stared at the skirt. 'You let me know if there's anything at all we can do to make your visit more comfortable.'

She returned to her conversation and strode out of the room.

'We best be going. Are you ready for the party of the year?' said Poppy, as if nothing out of the ordinary had happened.

Mayhem at the Mansion
Ch 21

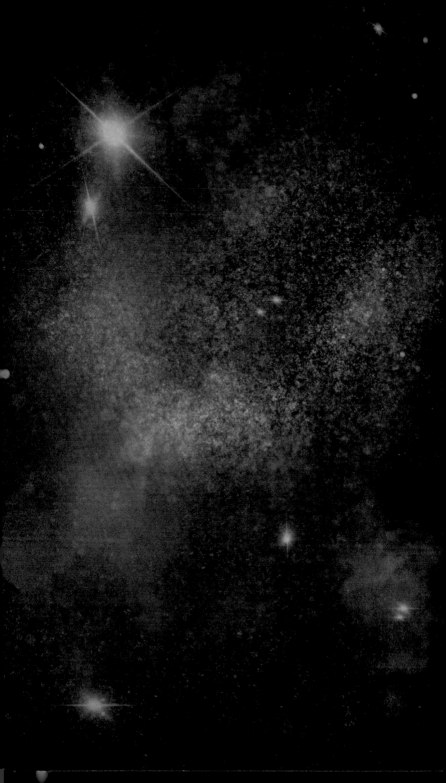

Cali could hear the noise of the crowd that had gathered in the hallway as they stood together at the top of the stairs.

Poppy grabbed her hand excitedly and turned to face her. 'Are you ready to make a grand entrance?'

Cali nodded. As they walked down the stairs, music started to play. Cali could feel the eyes of the entire year group on them. The large floor-to-ceiling glass doors that lined the back of the house were pulled back by waiters dressed in white, to allow the crowd to filter outside into the landscaped garden that housed a swimming pool surrounded by flowers and tall, exotic trees.

Cali couldn't believe her eyes. It felt like she'd walked into a music video, only without the models and celebrities. There was a DJ playing the decks, waitresses on roller skates weaving around the crowds with trays of mocktails, a bubble machine, a sweet cart, and a photo booth.

Poppy walked confidently towards the crowd. She turned to Cali. 'I'm going to have to leave you now and do my hostess bit.'

'Sure, no problem.' Cali scanned the garden for a familiar face in the sea of people. She failed to recognise anyone at all, which wasn't surprising. She'd only been at the school two minutes before she'd been suspended. Cali was sure people were whispering about her, or was it her imagination? She'd decided to go check out the mocktails when she bumped into the American boy from her science class.

'Hey, isn't this the second time you've run into me like this?' he said with a cheeky smile.

'Ha, yeah, I can be kind of clumsy.'

'I'm surprised to see you here. If the rumours are true, you and Poppy are like arch-enemies, or am I wrong?' He looked genuinely confused.

'It's complicated.' Cali scanned the room to avoid his direct gaze. She finally spotted Zia, who was first in line for candyfloss. She was just about to take a huge bite when their eyes met and she came rushing over.

'Cali, can you believe all this?' Zia opened her arms out wide. 'Hey, Nate. I might have to deflect to the dark side, so I can hang out here. Have you seen the chill-out area? They have a hot tub and these really cool hammocks. You can just find me hanging there for, like, the rest of my life,' she giggled.

'Anyway, I'm going to find the boys,' Nate interrupted. 'See you around.'

'Sure, see you,' Cali replied, pulling a face at Zia and trying to hold in a giggle.

'It's so obvious you like him,' Zia laughed. She looked her up and down. 'Nice skirt! Are you okay? I'm surprised you're still in one piece. So, Poppy hasn't tried to expose you, lock you in a cupboard or frame you with stolen goods yet? Things are going well. Better than last week.'

Cali laughed nervously. 'Actually, she's been okay. She let me wear her clothes and use her make-up. We're not going to be best friends or anything, but I feel like she's making an effort.'

'Well, don't let your guard down. The night is far from over, and if I know Poppy, she's not going to be able to resist this opportunity to put you in your place once and for all. My mum's on high alert, you know, she insisted on coming.'

'Girls and boys, can I have your attention please?' Mrs Delongue appeared in the middle of the crowd. She wore a camel-coloured dress with matching patent shoes and bag. Chunky gold jewellery hung around her tanned, wrinkled neck, and her blonde hair was freshly blow-dried. 'Thank you for joining us for the Crestview annual charity ball. It's wonderful to welcome so many old and new faces.

We'll be starting the auction at seven o'clock. In the meantime, enjoy.' She raised a glass of bubbly and flashed her bright white teeth.

Zia and Cali went off to explore. They got peach-flavoured mojitos with straws and sparklers. They danced a little at the edge of the dancefloor then found themselves two hammocks tucked away a little further down the garden, which were harder to get into than they looked. They had the perfect spot away from the chaos, but still with a good enough view of what was going on. They laid back and looked up at the full moon that lit up the evening sky.

'What do you think is really going on here?' Zia asked, raising one of her eyebrows. 'Is this some 'look, now, I'm friends with a mixed kid, so we can't possibly be racist' cover up? Or is this some scheme of Poppy's to really get to you, big time?'

'To be honest, I don't have a clue. You want to know something? It might sound a little crazy, but I know that the goddesses have my back.'

Zia looked at Cali and smiled. 'Oh, it's like that, is it? Is this to do with that game you mentioned before? The kingdom...no, sorry, The Queendom, wasn't it?'

'Yes, exactly! The Queendom.' Cali was pleased she'd remembered. 'I'm beginning to realise that the darkness is not so scary. We all have our inner demons, and it's much better to face them than to ignore them and let them take over.'

'Wow. That sounds deep, Cali.'

'It was. I mean, it is. I guess you could say I've started to embrace my inner witch as well as my inner goddess.'

'This still sounds kind of insane, but I'm beginning to learn not to expect anything less from you,' Zia laughed.

'Witches are not what you think they are. They can actually bend and shift reality and are the biggest rebels ever.'

'Okay, now you're talking. I'm in. So, when are you going to get me an invite to this game?'

'Really? I'll send you one, of course. I mean, I think you'd love it. You can be in my tribe.' Cali smiled, thinking how amazing it would be to share it all with someone. 'But, right now, I need to go to the bathroom. You coming?'

'Yeah, sure. You can tell me all about your inner witch and see if I've got what it takes to be one too.' They walked back to the house, past a group of girls huddled together with their phones out, comparing the contents of their screens. As soon as Cali walked by, the girls started laughing.

They found the bathroom near the kitchen, which, annoyingly, had a queue of four girls, who were chatting and laughing. As Cali and Zia approached, they all turned and stared.

'I'm starting to get the feeling something's going on that we don't know about.' Zia grabbed her phone from her bag. She scrolled through her social media alerts then suddenly stopped.

'Oh, God, Cali, no wonder. The whole year group has seen you in your underwear.' She flashed the phone in Cali's face. There was a photo of Poppy, looking every inch the model, next to Cali in her mismatched knickers and bra, looking terrified.

'I have to say, it's not the most flattering photo of you, but...' Zia said with a smile.

Cali looked at the image and immediately felt adrenaline flood her system. She was shocked, angry, hurt, confused and exposed; the emotions all §competing for her attention.

'I need to find Poppy, and I need to do this alone, Zia' she shouted above the music, before running off.

Poppy was in the middle of the dancefloor, moving to the beat of the music. She continually looked to see who was watching and made the most of every bit of attention, as though it fuelled her dance moves. From across the room, Cali saw her grab Nate's arm and pull out her phone.

It was as if someone hit the remote. Everything went into slow motion. Cali stormed through the crowd towards her. Poppy looked up, saw her coming and leaned closer to Nate as she swiped through her phone. 'Look who it is! Hey, Cali, are you enjoying the party?' She twirled around her and reached out for her hands. Cali pulled them away, incensed.

'I need to speak to you in private.' Cali's heart beat furiously. It felt like it could rip through her t-shirt and jump right out of her chest. Instead, it found its way to her throat; it sat there, booming away, almost blocking her words.

'Whatever you have to say to me can be said right here. We're among friends,' Poppy sniggered. She smiled at Nate, who looked increasingly confused and uncomfortable.

'Just stop the act, Poppy. It's all just a show for you, isn't it? It's all fake. Your whole life is about what it looks like on the outside to everyone else.'

'That sounds like a touch of badly-disguised jealousy to me,' Poppy retorted.

'I've seen it.'

'Seen what?' she asked, innocently. Cali felt her anger churn in the pit of her stomach and worried about the potential explosion. People around them were beginning to stare and strain their heads as they danced, to try and work out what was going on. 'Oh, our selfie? You look super-hot, why wouldn't you want to show off a body like that?'

'That's bullshit and you know it! You've no right to post any photo of me without my consent, especially not one in my underwear. Violating my privacy has serious consequences.'

'Come on, Cali, it's only on my stories. It'll be gone before you know it.'

'Remove it right now!' Cali demanded.

'Are you going to make me?' Poppy asked with a provocative pout.

That was the last straw for Cali. A concoction of emotions fuelled her forwards. She lunged towards Poppy and managed to swipe the phone from her hands. Cali noted the shock on the faces of Poppy, Martha, and her inner circle, who were gathered around them. As Cali landed on the floor, feeling triumphant, she heard a loud ripping sound. A sense of dread instantly filled her belly like lead. As she got to her feet, Cali looked down to see Poppy's skirt hanging off her, exposing her backside to the whole room. In that moment, Cali wished harder than she'd ever wished before - for the floor to open up and swallow her whole, so that she was never seen again.

'What have you done? You stupid idiot!' Poppy shrieked. Her face had turned a deep shade of crimson and her eyes had a demonic look to them. 'Your fat arse has just destroyed a thousand-pound, limited edition skirt - it cost more than you're worth!'

Poppy's penetrating blue eyes projected beams of intense hate, which pierced Cali's energy field and broke through the barrier of her soft, caramel skin, travelling straight to the centre of her heart.

Poppy leaned in close. 'Oh, darling, did you really think we were going to be friends?'

Her words wrapped around Cali like long, weedy tendrils full of spiky thorns. Every time she tried to get away, she felt them pierce her again and again. 'Goddess, it's hurting,' she cried, deep inside, as the well of emotion in her belly began to swirl then overflow. The energy couldn't stay inside, it was too intense - so it erupted. It flowed up and out in a fountain of tears, leaving her gasping for air.

'Oh dear, have I said something to upset you? You seem to be a little emotional, just like your crazy mother.'

Then came the laughter. Big belly laughs, high-pitched squeals and staccato sniggers. Cali didn't think it was possible, but the laughter hurt even more than the harsh, cold looks and the mean words. In the face of those fresh, innocent tears, the laughter was cruel and mocking. Cali ordered the tears to retreat, but it was no use, they were in full flow now. She struggled to take back control of her body...the body that always betrayed her. 'Stop!' Cali yelled inside her head.

Stop embarrassing me. Why do you always have to do this? You've been exposed. See, they're right, you are weak, you're an embarrassment. You need to toughen up, you're useless. I wish I wasn't me.

'Why are you doing this to me? What do you want from me?' Cali whimpered.

All of a sudden, it felt like light was projecting outwards from the centre of her navel. Cali felt power surging through her body. *Please don't let it happen, not here, not now.* Her powers had got her in enough trouble, now they were actually going to expose her in front of the whole school, and she had no way of controlling or stopping them.

'Listen to me carefully,' Poppy said. 'I'm doing this because you should know better than to mess with me. If you try anything or step out of line again, believe me, you'll wish you were dead. Which is pretty much what we all wish you were, anyway.'

Everything went hazy for Cali, as though she was looking at the scene through a car-wash. She could see them all, standing around, circling her, watching her, laughing at her, talking about her. They were enjoying this. In her imagination, they were closing in, snarling like a pack of wild wolves that wanted to rip her to shreds with their teeth. She could feel her powers had been activated, there was no turning back. It was like a runaway train that could not be stopped. It was going to expose her.

All Cali ever wanted was to fit in, to be accepted for being herself. It was so unfair. Like playing some cruel game that you could never turn off or come out of. She would give anything to live in the world the goddesses described, the golden age, where everyone was connected and lived in harmony. But that world didn't exist, not even in The Queendom. This was the real world, a world Cali felt she couldn't be a part of.

Shifting Reality
Ch 22

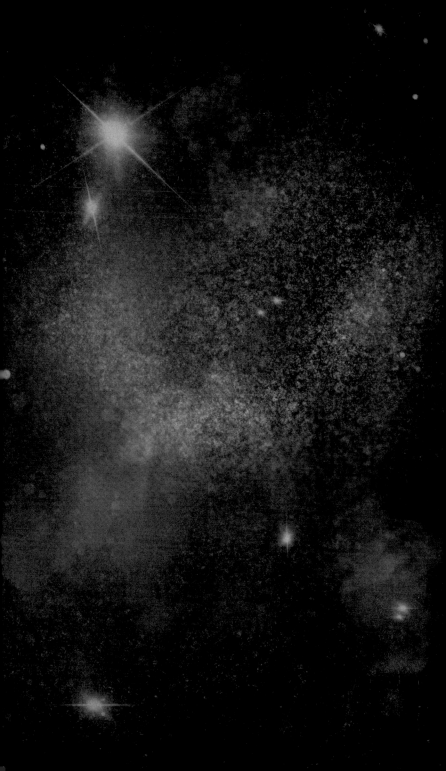

'*It's as easy as ABC. Come into your heart and switch your perspective,*' a voice commanded. '*Activate your awareness. Anchor your body with your breathing. Create inner calm, so that you can connect with clarity to your heart and higher wisdom.*'

Cali woke up on a different side of reality and began to slow her shallow breathing. She could feel the sensations in her body as she became hyper-aware of everything around her in that moment. She brought her attention to her heart and felt all of her senses switch on. She imagined the ball of light energy surrounding and protecting her, and she repeated the mantra three times.

'I am safe, connected and protected. I'm not alone.'

When Cali looked at Poppy she was frozen with a snarl on her face and angry, squinting eyes. The sight reminded Cali of something Grandma Georgina used to say when she was little, whenever she pulled a sour face. 'Be careful, if the wind changes, your face will stay that way forever!' Well, it looked like the wind had finally changed. Just like magic, Poppy was captured for all eternity with all her ugly inner demons exposed. Cali looked all around her and realised that everything she could see was frozen, as if someone had pressed 'pause' on a remote control of life.

Cali felt herself begin to rise; slowly at first, so she was hovering just a few inches above the ground. Then, suddenly, she began to float towards the ceiling and she was able to look down at the scene below. Her fingers tried to hold on to something, but there was nothing but air.

'*Surrender,*' a voice said.

Cali heard the command, and even though her mind argued and wanted to resist the unfamiliar sensation, she felt her whole body go soft. The more she let go, the higher she rose, up towards the

211

skylight that allowed the light of the full moon to spill in. Out into the vast, starry night sky, up she floated, safe within her protective bubble. Air rushed past her as she flew higher and higher, faster and faster, into the sky, through a pink mist, until she reached an iridescent light, which was when her bubble dissolved around her. Cali was suspended in mid-air, yet she felt supported and free as she floated down through the cosmos, surrounded by the bright light. This was what she imagined heaven must be like. The light was so radiant, she couldn't imagine it belonged to the world she knew.

Once her eyes became accustomed to the brightness, they started to bring a familiar outline into focus. Cali couldn't believe it, the temple from The Queendom was right there in front of her. It was even more magnificent to see the astral structure in real life, standing upon purple-tinged clouds above her head. Cali stared at the temple with amazement and awe. It was as if someone had drawn the outline of a building with strobes of light. What would have been walls were suspended structures of glistening crystals and shining stars. There was a ripple in the atmosphere and Eset appeared with her feet cushioned on a cloud. Eset's wings were spread wide, so that each vibrant turquoise feather glistened with a metallic sheen as she rose up in front of her. The goddess swept Cali up in a warm embrace. Cali could feel her strong arms and feathery wings wrapping her in so much love that it sent shivers throughout her body. Then Eset's distinctive voice, soft as a feather yet powerful as thunder, filled the space. 'Relax, Cali, let go of anything you thought you knew. You're so loved and supported. You are light.'

Cali's mind was reeling. She didn't understand what was happening. Just a minute ago, she was in Poppy's mansion, about to lose control of her power and expose herself in front of the whole school, and now she was here, in The Queendom, surrounded by light, in the presence of an actual goddess. Cali had so many questions, yet the shock made her speechless. *Was she dreaming?* she wondered. *Had she fainted or collapsed?*

'You're not imagining this. Your willingness to heal transcends all barriers. You have called on the goddesses and we have answered. By connecting to your higher self before reacting from a place of hurt you were able to channel your power to pause time and allow us to help you shape reality.' Eset clicked her fingers and Bast appeared to her left. The young goddess was even more beautiful in the flesh. She smiled warmly at Cali. Then Eset clicked her fingers again and the Dark Goddess, Hecate, appeared to her right. Everything about Hecate's presence epitomised the shadow - her dark eyes and hooded gown. This time, instead of being afraid, Cali noticed how her energy felt intensely protective. Cali automatically bowed her head, feeling grateful for all they had taught her.

Eset clicked her fingers a third time and they were all instantly transported to Poppy's mansion. The three goddesses created a trio of light that formed a triangle around the scene at the party, frozen in time.

'We're ready to begin. Bast will provide protection, Hecate will support your shadow work, and I will bring the healing light.' Eset opened and spread her wings so that they filled the space. When she held out her hands, a strobe of bright white light could be seen in her palms. Bast shapeshifted into her feline form then flapped her beautiful wings to fly in a circle around the scene, until she'd created an iridescent light bubble around the whole house.

'Hey, girl, we have work to do, but you know we all have your back.'

Hecate stepped forward. She held dried flowers,

213

herbs and glass bottles of potions in her hands.
'Now, I will help you integrate the shadow. First, you
must honour your pain. Tell me what you're feeling.'
Cali closed her eyes, as she brought back the exact
moment she felt the shock.

'I feel betrayed, scared, like an outsider, like I
don't belong. I feel like I'll be attacked. I feel angry at
Poppy and angry at myself. I feel stupid for trusting,
silly for believing. I feel abandoned and upset at my
mum for getting me into this mess.'

'Good work. It's okay to feel these emotions. Tell
me what it looks like and where it is in your body,'
said Hecate.

'What, like it's an actual thing?' Cali asked.

'Yes. Look closely and tell me what you see,' Hecate
answered, opening one of the glass bottles and
sprinkling its contents over Cali's head. Cali felt the
emotion in her chest and was surprised that she
could actually see something when she looked down.

'Okay, this is weird. It's a big, dark, solid mass of
swirling energy. It's as heavy as concrete with dark,
sticky tendrils hooked around my heart, stuck to my
entire chest.'

'Good, Cali. Does this mass of dark energy have a
message for you?'

Cali looked confused at the question. 'Hang on a
minute, I can actually speak to this thing inside of
me?'

'Yes, it's trauma. Old, painful emotions that have
become trapped in the body. It wants to be felt and
freed. So, yes, with practice, it will communicate with
you.'

'Okay. I guess I'll ask it.' Cali looked at the
swirling, dark mass and when she asked, she was
surprised by its response. 'It's not safe to be me.'

Hecate held out her hand to reach Cali's. 'You're
doing so well. Shadow work is not for the faint-
hearted. Some of the pain you feel is not just yours,

it's pain that has been passed down your ancestral line, from your mother, your grandmother, your great grandmother.' As Hecate spoke, seven women appeared, forming a line behind Cali. Their outlines were faint and a little hazy.

Cali didn't know the woman at the far end of the line, but she had the same heavy, grey, swirling mass of energy inside her. She reached to gather it then she passed it to the next woman, and the next woman, until Cali recognised her grandmother holding it and passing it to her mother, and finally, her mother handing it to her.

'You're seeing how women have had to suffer in silence for centuries. How they have had to conform to fit in. How they have given up pieces of themselves. They have been betrayed, hurt, and stripped of their power. Often, the only thing they could do was swallow their pain deep inside.' In that moment, Cali started to realise that things weren't quite as simple as she'd thought. Maybe all of this wasn't her mum's fault.

Eset stepped forward and held out her hands. Light began to stream out from both palms, surrounding Cali and all of the women. 'You are the chosen one. It takes someone with true courage to walk the path of the healer and break generational curses, but once you do, everyone can be healed and freed.'

Cali studied the women, whose clothing was so drastically different and demonstrated the different eras in time they each came from. The features on their faces, however, seemed so familiar.

'Now, let's use the light to gather any other shadow energy and remove it from your body and your aura. Watch it swirl and collect as it leaves, to be returned to love.'

Cali watched as the light from Eset's hands flooded out and into her body, filling every cell of her being with glorious, white dazzling light. It infiltrated the

215

mass of heavy grey energy, and she watched as it began to dissolve; it was then swept up and cleared from her system. As it disappeared, Cali saw the light travel down the line. One by one, it entered the bodies of her ancestors and allowed the stuck energy to vanish from them, too. She felt the strength of this invisible army of women around her, and the beauty of it made her cry. Eset smiled and the light from her hands retracted.

'Let's look at Poppy. In many ways, she's your mirror,' Hecate said, stepping forward once again. 'What do you want to ask her? In this moment, you'll be able to speak directly to her higher self and access her inner truth.'

Cali didn't have to think twice. 'Why are you doing this to me? What do you want from me? Why do you wish I was dead?'

Poppy's features softened. She looked at the scene around her, then at Cali and the goddesses, and she began to cry. Her chest heaved as waves of emotion took over.

'The light in you frightens me. I've been taught to fear it, because it exposes my own shadow. I must protect myself by hurting others. I stop them from getting close, or they'll see what I'm hiding. I'm not worthy of love and attention. I'm scared that I'm unlovable. I've been alone for way too long.'

As Poppy spoke, Cali saw a completely different quality light up her face. She was just a girl with the same fears as her, and the same mixed-up emotions running through her body. Hecate smiled. She pulled out the red jasper crystal that hovered above Poppy's head.

'Look closer. Do you see the shadow lodged in her aura?' asked Hecate.

Cali watched as the crystal illuminated her aura, allowing it to be seen. There were colourful layers surrounding her body. The energy moved like it was breathing and pulsating, getting brighter then dimmer. In parts close to her heart, Cali could see dark spots, like tears.

'She has a unique ancestral line. You can see the same in her mother.' Hecate rattled her keys and they were able to zoom in on Poppy's mum, who was standing at the centre of a large crowd with a champagne glass in her hand. She had exactly the same rips in her aura, except the darkness of her shadow created bigger blocks that obscured most of the colours, which were faint.

'You will get an opportunity to heal some aspect of this. Use your red jasper crystal, it will help cleanse her aura,' Hecate suggested.

Eset stepped forward. 'Let's move into the light work. You see how her pain has been passed down through generations? It brings a message. What we really need to ask is, what is this trying to show me? What does this have to teach me? This situation shows how, even when we seem so separate, we're really connected. We have the same fears.'

'Yes, I guess I can see how we both feel alone and abandoned in some way by what's happened to us,' said Cali.

'It's important to remember that you always have a choice. You can be triggered by fear and react in a way that separates you further, or you can choose love and be the light. One option chains you to your pain, the other sets you free.' Eset opened her hands and the crystals hovered above her palms. 'Our time is coming to an end. Be proud of what you have achieved here. Remember, the healing journey is like a spiral; we often have to revisit situations with new awareness and ways of being. This is just the beginning, Cali, there's so much more work to do, so be sure to come back to The Queendom soon.'

The three goddesses moved together to hold hands then they rose into the air. A powerful golden light glowed from their centres, which spread out until it covered their entire bodies. Then, as fast as they'd appeared, they were gone and Cali was back in the room, face to face with Poppy. The girl who had gone out of her way to make Cali's life painful because she was desperately hiding her own pain. Cali looked into Poppy's scowling eyes. She bypassed the intimidation and saw the same glimmer of truth she'd discovered earlier. She searched for the connection to her heart, took a deep breath, and in a voice that was just a little louder than a whisper, she said, 'I know what it feels like to be scared you're not loved.'

The words stopped Poppy in her tracks. She stared at Cali with a look of confusion. She paused for a moment, almost as if she was searching for recognition. Then came the flow of tears, which seemed to both shock and horrify Poppy. She ran through the crowd, hiding her face in her hands and knocking people out of the way. She ran right past her mother, who looked up momentarily from the group of people hanging on her every word.

'Girls are so emotional at this age,' Mrs Delongue commented, raising an eyebrow and shaking her head dismissively, before returning to her conversation.

Seven Generations
Ch 23

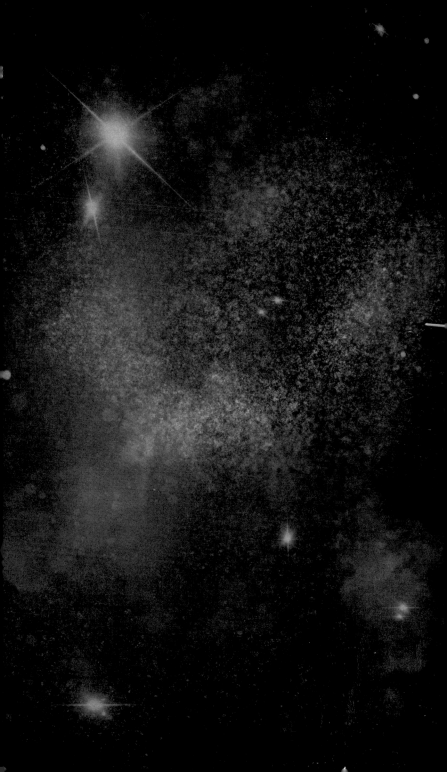

'What just happened there?' said Zia.

'You wouldn't believe it if I told you,' Cali responded. Looking over Zia's shoulder, she realised Poppy's friends were still gathered around them, staring angrily at her.

'What did you say to Poppy to upset her like that, you little witch?' seethed Martha, her face inches from Cali's. Zia's mum appeared, having seen the confrontation from the other side of the room. Her presence made Martha and the other girls turn around and pretend to be chatting among themselves.

'Is everything alright, girls?' Ms Ombassu asked, putting a hand on each of their shoulders. 'Cali, your skirt is torn!' she exclaimed.

Zia stood behind Cali, in an attempt to protect her modesty.

'Here, I have some safety pins that might hold it together.' Zia's mum rummaged through her bag then bent down to pin the gaping skirt. She looked at the two of them for some kind of explanation but was met with blank faces. 'Perhaps it's time for us to leave. I'll just say goodbye to the other teachers and bring the car round. I'll meet you out front in ten minutes, no longer.'

'Okay, Mum,' Zia replied. They watched as she made her way through the crowd before turning to each other and releasing a collective sigh.

'I didn't know what to say then. What's going on, Cali? Can you let me in on what the hell is happening?'

'I promise I will, but I need to get my bag first. I'll meet you at the entrance.'

'Want me to come with you?' Zia asked, a concerned look on her face.

'No, honestly, I'll be fine. I'll meet you out front,' she said, giving her a hug.

Just as Cali headed towards the sea of people, she felt a hand gently grab her arm. She turned and saw Nate. 'Hey. Are you okay?' he asked, a genuine look of concern on his face.

'Yeah, I'm fine. Mortally embarrassed, but fine.' Cali felt heat in her body rise. She avoided his gaze in the hope he wouldn't notice.

'Just for the record, I don't think it's you that should be embarrassed. You handled that really well.' He looked downwards with a mischievous grin. 'Actually, I like the skirt. You might start a trend. It's kind of cool retro punk!'

'Stranger things have happened,' Cali replied, unable to stop a smile from reaching her lips. It vanished when she remembered where she was headed. 'I've, err, got to go get my things.' She kept her bottom and the torn skirt as close to the wall as possible as she rushed past him.

She ran up the main staircase and walked quietly down the corridor to Poppy's bedroom. When she was just outside the door, she could hear screaming and banging coming from inside. She entered cautiously. She couldn't see Poppy, but realised that the noise was coming from the walk in wardrobe. As Cali entered, she instinctively ducked to avoid being hit by a flying handbag. Poppy was sitting on one of the shelves in the middle of the wardrobe, the spotlights highlighting her red, puffy face. Even Cali's appearance didn't stop her from letting out an angry growl as she continued to throw her bags, one by one, across the room.

'Hey,' Cali said, backing into the doorway for safety. 'Can I just say, I think you have every right to be angry. I actually think I'd feel the same if I was you.'

'How could you ever know what it's like to be me?' asked Poppy.

Cali took a breath, came into her heart and

protected herself energetically, knowing that, as tempting as it was to react with the same anger, she could choose a different way.

'Maybe underneath the fancy clothes and handbags, we're more similar than you think.' Cali reached for the plastic bag on the floor that held her things. As she bent down to grab it, she felt a heat coming from the crystals she'd tucked in her bra. Cali pulled them out and watched as the deep red jasper one floated above her hand.

Poppy stopped crying and looked up, in shock, at the sight before her. Cali stood in the centre of the room, in awe of the red crystal hovering in midair. The most beautiful white light shone from Cali's palms.

She instinctively recited her mantra and, remembering Hecate's words, focused her attention on the white light of her energy ball; she expanded it until it surrounded Poppy's aura. 'I am connected and protected. I am not alone.'

She heard someone enter the bedroom. 'Cali? Are you in there?'

It was Zia. She cautiously peered around the door, only to be met by the illuminated scene. 'Woah!' she remarked. Speechlessly, she watched Cali and Poppy become completely encapsulated in the glowing white light.

Cali kept her focus on Poppy and spoke clearly. 'What do you need to release, Poppy? It's safe to let it go. Give it to the crystal.' Poppy remained silent. Her eyes were wide as she looked up and down in total awe at the light surrounding her.

'It's okay, you don't need to do anything,' Cali said, gaining confidence. 'Just remain open. I'm sensing the fear inside you. The crystal will help you release any emotional bullying you're experiencing.'

Poppy remained frozen and didn't utter a word.

'Watch the crystal as the emotion clears,' Cali said

223

softly.

The glowing red crystal swept around Poppy's body and collected the dark shadows that were lodged there, mending the rips and tears as it moved. Poppy closed her eyes and, as the crystal made its way back to Cali's hands, a look of peace washed over her face, softening her features and making her cheeks glow. Cali smiled at Zia, who had been silent for the longest amount of time since she'd known her. As the light around the two girls retracted, the room returned to its normal state.

'I told you,' Poppy stammered. 'I told you she's a witch.'

'Wow, Cali. Like, wow!' Zia remarked. 'That was out of this world incredible. You've got powers, after all. Girl, you need to embrace them to the max!'

'Let's get out of here,' Cali said with a smile, grabbing Zia's arm.

As they got to the bedroom doorway, Poppy called out. 'Cali, just so you know. I've removed the video and I'm... I'm... don't worry about the skirt.'

Cali didn't look back. Instead, she lifted her eyes to the heavens, took a deep breath and smiled.

As they drove home, no one spoke until Ms Ombassu broke the silence. 'Well, girls, what a way to end the term. I can't say I'm surprised by the evening's turn of events. She looked in the rear view mirror at the two girls on the back seat. 'By the look of it, you handled it well, Cali. You should be proud of yourself for making the most of a difficult situation.'

'Actually, I'd like to thank you for always coming to my rescue, Ms Ombassu,' Cali giggled, relieved to be in the company of people who understood her.

'Call me Milika. From what I saw this evening, there's definitely no rescuing required. Building resilience is a necessity in our world these days. We can't often choose what happens to us, but we can always choose how we react.'

Cali felt that this was something the goddesses would say. She noticed how she always felt safe in Zia's and her mum's presence. They had that same grounding energy.

'What did you say to her, though?' asked Zia. 'I mean, it was like you totally disarmed her with your words. I've never seen her react like that before. It was cool!'

'Zia, you're talking about someone's pain here, don't make fun,' Ms Ombassu retorted, 'Even though she can be pretty despicable at times, she's still a human being.'

Zia mouthed to Cali to text her later, giving her friend a pinch as she stifled a laugh.

'Who's going to be there when you get home, Cali?' Ms Ombassu asked.

'My mum and my grandma. She's been staying over while my dad's working abroad,' Cali answered awkwardly, hoping that Ms Ombassu wouldn't ask any more questions.

Ms Ombassu seemed to sense Cali's unease. She turned the radio up a notch, so that it provided a cover for the girls to chat. Cali felt a vibration and pulled the phone out of her pocket.

The Queendom: *Congratulations! You have succeeded in embracing your shadow, you've gained your first key and opened the red vortex closest to Earth.*

You have also connected to the goddesses in all three worlds. You've gained your second key that will open the violet vortex closest to heaven.

This means you have unlocked access to the next level of the game. We can't wait to welcome you back to The Queendom to give you your next mission and introduce you to your sisterhood.

Blessings, Eset.

Now Cali knew that the game and the goddesses

were so much more than some kind of fantasy,
nothing in the world would keep her away.

'Is everything okay, Cali?' Ms Ombassu asked,
noticing her reaction to the message.

'Yes, it is. Everything finally feels like it's going to
be okay,' Cali replied, smiling at Zia. She grabbed her
friend's hand and squeezed it tightly.

*

Arriving home, Cali closed the door behind her
quietly. She paused in the hallway for a moment
to gather her breath. She could hear the TV in the
living room and her mum and grandma talking in
low voices. She'd prayed that they'd both be in bed,
so she wouldn't have to stand there awkwardly
and censor her recollection of the entire evening,
to pretend it was something different than what it
was. Cali took off her shoes and tiptoed past the big
mirror that hung on the wall near the shoe stand.
She glanced at her reflection and thought she saw
the outline of three people standing behind her,
gesturing for her to enter the living room. When she
looked again, no one was there.

'Cali, we're in here,' her mum called. Cali peered
round the door to see her grandma sat in her dad's
armchair and her mum laid on the sofa with Rocco
curled up like a fox near her feet. As soon as he saw
Cali, he jumped down to greet her with a little bark
and a big, slobbery kiss.

'So, how was the party?' her mum asked eagerly.
'And where did you get that skirt from?' She peered
closer. 'Are you okay, baby? Did something happen
that you want to talk about?'

Cali stared at her with suspicion.

'Come and sit down. Do you want a nice hot
chocolate?' She patted the blue velvet sofa.

'No, Mum, it's okay. I'm fine.'

'So...how was it?'

'Let's just say it was interesting,' Cali said.

'Hmm, that doesn't sound like a good kind of interesting, but it's okay if you don't want to talk about it. In fact, I get it, I know I probably haven't been the easiest person to have a conversation with lately.' She looked at Grandma Georgina then turned back to Cali.

'Whatever happened, it feels like something heavy has shifted. Actually, Grandma and I want to talk to you,' she said awkwardly. Grandma Georgina passed her the carved wooden box that Cali found in her room. It was the box containing the ankh.

'In fact, there's so much we need to tell you, and it's time you knew the truth. We have powers but we're not able to control them.' Cali gawked. She sat down and looked from her mum to her grandma and back again. The silence rested heavily over them, like a thick blanket.

Her grandma spoke in a low voice that almost cracked. 'When I was a little girl, my grandmother had a special gift. She could talk to spirits. I remember her as a warm, comforting woman to whom I could say anything. I was only eleven when she was put on trial, charged with witchcraft and sent to prison, after being branded a witch. The news spread around the small village where we lived like wildfire.' Grandma shook her head and Cali's mum looked just as shocked as she did at the revelation.

'Don't you think it would have been helpful to have explained this to me when I was expelled from school?' Cali's mum asked, a hurt look in her eyes. 'That maybe, instead of punishing me for not being a good girl, you could have told me this story back then?'

'Hang on a minute,' said Cali. 'You were expelled from school too? And you didn't think of telling me? Can you hear yourself?'

'Please stop,' Grandma Georgina interrupted. 'Don't you understand? We all suffer by keeping this in the shadows. We thought we were protecting you, just as my parents thought they were protecting me. Listen to me. The truth has to be heard now.' She paused and pulled Cali to her. 'My dad had to teach me how to box, as I'd come home from school with scratches and bruises. I got so much abuse in the playground. I was called 'evil eye' and 'witch spawn'. You name it. Children can be so cruel, as you well know. My mother shut it out of her mind completely and we were never allowed to mention it, but the stigma in our family has followed us ever since. She was just an ordinary woman with a gift.' Her voice was solemn.

Cali wasn't sure if she was still breathing when her grandma stopped talking. She couldn't work out how she was here, in this moment, actually hearing these words, nor the path that had led her to them. In her mind's eye, time went back to the very beginning of her journey. Cali saw the book laid open in the library, she remembered how she'd been led to the game, how she'd encountered the goddesses, all she'd learned about her gifts, and how she'd come face to face with the witch. She'd gone from fearing her to embracing her. Witchcraft was in her bloodline, in both her ancestry and her destiny. Could it be that this path was just waiting for her all this time? That the game was so much more than just a game?

Cali looked at her mum and her grandma in a completely different way and felt the presence of the goddesses fill the room. Rocco jumped up, tilted his head to one side and began to bark and whimper as he looked towards the centre of the room. Cali was sure they all felt them.

'Maybe we're just ordinary girls and women with extraordinary gifts,' said Cali.

The ankh

'Gifts that cannot be denied or hidden anymore.'
Cali's Grandma added. 'Gifts that can't be shrouded
by secrets and lies. Gifts that are ready to come out
of the shadows.'

The three of them moved closer, reaching out
their arms to hold one another. Three generations
coming together in a strong embrace. Cali's mum
took hold of both Cali and her own mother's hand
and looked into their eyes. 'We can't move forward
unless we clear up the past,' she said. 'For the first
time in a long while I believe there's new hope. A way
for the girls and women in this family to embrace
their powers and finally accept that they're truly
extraordinary.'

THE END

About the Author

Jo Stevenson is an artist, writer, Kundalini yoga and meditation teacher; coach, healer and mama of two beautiful mixed-race girls. She is on a mission to inspire women and girls to celebrate their unique beauty and stand in their own power in a society that wants to tell them differently.

After spending almost two decades in London in a corporate career as a clever way to hide from her big creative dreams, she thankfully found a safe sisterhood and Kundalini yoga, which awakened her sleeping creativity.

During meditation, Jo saw a vision of a woman with beautiful gold and turquoise wings and she was slain. It was only later, with the help of Google, that she realised she was a goddess. This marked the start of a magical journey. Jo made a deal with the goddess to tell her story, and as she did, over time, they were both able to heal and rise.

Jo now lives in her hometown in Yorkshire with her husband, two daughters and two dogs. She still loves to teach yoga, paint bright pictures, and find a little time each day to connect with the goddess.

'The goddess has your back' is Jo's debut novel and first book in the series 'Soul Star Sisters'.

www.jostevensoncreative.co.uk

Gratitude

The story of the book is almost as magical as the story contained here within these pages. There are many angels, guides, guardians and goddesses in both the earthly and heavenly realms that have helped me to bring it into being andI am eternally grateful to each and everyone of them.

Seven years ago I met a a kindred spirit who was really a goddess in disguise. She opened up a whole new world to me and although she grew real wings and left this world too soon I have always felt her spirit supporting my work at each step of the journey. This book is my creative offering to honour your spirit Collette Hughes, you are always in our hearts. Love always to Ruby and John.

To Anna Lempriere, my greatest teacher, biggest cheerleader and most inspirational guide. None of this would be possible without you. You met me when I was lost, at my darkest, lowest point and gently guided me home. You gave me six weeks to finish this story seven years ago and I wrote every night and produced 60,000 words that have since become the basis of this whole series. Thank you for all you do. I love you and am eternally grateful.

Thank you to Trevor Simon-Spooner who was the only other person I ever shared my work with for many years. Your patience, humour, hand holding and arse kicking have always been exactly what I've needed.

To my incredible coach Emily Tamayo Maher who has worked with me on the minute detail of this book and has supported and encouraged me to keep going when I felt I couldn't.

To the inedibly talented Freya Rose Ellis who brought Cali and the Queendom to life in the most magical ways and to Vân Dang for all your brilliant, meticulous design.

To Fay Garrett for your support, ideas and feedback, to Verity Watts for holding my hand through the last hurdles. To all the beta readers who have taken their time to give feedback - My super duper sis, Nicola Gilbert, Glenn Younger, Lisa Wolfe, Lindsey Maxfield. To Diane Hall and Joy Clacker for your fabulous proof reading and polishing.

So much gratitude to all my IE sisters, especially to my wonderful mentor Tash Mitch, your connection to the goddess, guidance, wisdom and way you hold space has allowed me to blossom in the most magical ways.

In writing this story I have often been asked to walk the exact path of the heroine and to face my shadows along the way. To so many of my soul sisters and beautiful friends that have supported me and held me as I have done so I owe a lot. You have listened to my dreams about the story for many years and I deeply appreciate your love and support - Melinda Gerrard, Julie Adams, Kate Tiffany, Lisa Bethlehem, Fiona Hughes, Abena Akohene, Lisa Di Mambro, Laura Birch, Sarah Wadsworth, Karen Pernyes, Leanne Marie, Judith Brook, Mary-Kate Fallon-Smith, Kelly Be, Sian Pillay.

To my dearest soul sister Milika Laveist who taught me the true meaning of sisterhood and encouraged me to celebrate every day and rise. I will continue to do so in your honour. I love you and miss you madly.

To the teachers and mentors that have inspired me and ignited my passion for story telling and the goddess though your workshops and offerings to the world - Somalia Seaton, Lisa Lister, Sophie Bashford, Yasmin Boland, Guru Jagat, Kari Samuels.

Big shout out my wonderful tribe of Kundalini yogis and Wakey Massives you know who you are!

To all the women in the many circles I move in thank you for allowing me to be seen, felt, heard and held.

Last but not least, love always to my wonderful crazy family, my mum Andrea who I'm delighted walks this path with me and my dad Geoff who has always encouraged me to be the best I can be, you have made me the woman I am today. Love to my brother Paul, Sarah and the kids, Elaine, John. To Grace, Dawn, Nash and Kai - love you like cooked food. Earl, Ashley, Olivia and Lola thank you for all that you are and bring to my life. I love you more than you could ever know.

Keep shining.

Jo x